Brier Hill

Jimmy Taaffe

Archway Publishing

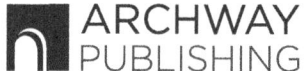

Copyright © 2023 Jimmy Taaffe.

All rights reserved. No part of this book may be used or reproduced by any means, graphic, electronic, or mechanical, including photocopying, recording, taping or by any information storage retrieval system without the written permission of the author except in the case of brief quotations embodied in critical articles and reviews.

Archway Publishing books may be ordered through booksellers or by contacting:

Archway Publishing
1663 Liberty Drive
Bloomington, IN 47403
www.archwaypublishing.com
844-669-3957

Because of the dynamic nature of the Internet, any web addresses or links contained in this book may have changed since publication and may no longer be valid. The views expressed in this work are solely those of the author and do not necessarily reflect the views of the publisher, and the publisher hereby disclaims any responsibility for them.

This is a work of fiction. All of the characters, names, incidents, organizations, and dialogue in this novel are either the products of the author's imagination or are used fictitiously.

Any people depicted in stock imagery provided by Getty Images are models, and such images are being used for illustrative purposes only. Certain stock imagery © Getty Images.

Inspired by true events

ISBN: 978-1-6657-5234-3 (sc)
ISBN: 978-1-6657-5235-0 (e)

Library of Congress Control Number: 2023920645

Print information available on the last page.

Archway Publishing rev. date: 10/31/2023

Brier Hill

PROLOGUE
APRIL 2024

The big yellow school bus pulled into the parking lot of the Youngstown History Center, full of students from Canfield Middle School.

"Boys and girls! Remember to wear your nametag and stick close together!" the seventh-grade teacher hollered over the excited children as they exited the bus.

The long line of children filed inside the History Center for their field trip. This might not have been the most exciting destination for a group of seventh-graders, but it sure beat sitting in Mrs. Fender's social studies class.

A cute volunteer college student from Youngstown State University took the children from exhibit to exhibit and spoke about various historical highlights of the Mahoning Valley. She explained each exhibit carefully and how it showcased a point in Youngstown history that was significant, interesting, or even a little fun.

The kids dashed up the stairs to the second story, where a massive display of all the Youngstown neighborhoods lined the side wall. Fosterville, Cottage Grove, Newport, Brier Hill, and so on.

Each display featured a large collage of old images from the turn of the century through the 1980s, as well as a colorful history of each neighborhood.

In a corner of the Brier Hill exhibit was an old, tattered photograph barely noticeable to anyone. It was slightly sun-faded, and the corner was missing with a crease down the middle. A little tag below the picture simply read: "Brier Hill, Circa 1977." Courtesy of the *Youngstown Vindicator* newspaper.

The photograph showed two twenty-something-year-old kids, who looked as if they were in the prime of their lives. They were standing in the street in front of a pizzeria whose sign on the window read, "LaVilla Pizza." The pizzeria is now long gone, of course, along with most of what was Brier Hill.

The girl had her arms around his waist, and they were both smiling grandly. He was clutching a stickball bat, and she was holding a bottle of grape soda.

Handwritten in the corner of the image in faded ballpoint pen, it said: Benny and Taffy June 1977. The little script was only visible if you looked closely.

The picture, like the Brier Hill neighborhood, is now just a ghost from a long-gone memory.

CHAPTER 1
TAFFY

In the spring of 1977, Taffy Centofanti, just twenty-three years old, was getting ready to open her little boutique soda parlor in the Brier Hill neighborhood of Youngstown, Ohio. Taffy smiled from the sidewalk, watching the old man meticulously make the fine brush dance on the store's front window. The calligraphy read in a dainty but large script: "Il Mio Piccolo Negozio Di Soda."

"Thank you, Mr. Donavito!" Taffy chimed cheerfully, rocking on her heels with her hands on her hips.

"You going to make a great business owner, Taffy girl. Your papa would be so proud," Mr. Donavito said in his thick Italian accent, taking a step back and inspecting his work.

Taffy beamed with pride at the little plaudit from Mr. Donavito. She skipped past him, giving his arm a small, affectionate squeeze as she stepped inside her new business.

The soda parlor smelled of fresh paint and new carpeting. While the new freezers and tables were still in their plastic wrap, the long counter and bar stools were neatly set up. Behind the counter, Taffy had a large Coca-Cola sign above the sink and eight vintage

1

Tiffany-style lamps hung from the tin ceiling. The little shop looked as if Norman Rockwell himself had helped Taffy decorate.

The centerpiece of the parlor was a large neon ice cream cone that hung in stark contrast to the bone-white walls. She had neatly placed jars of penny candy that lined the counter from end to end. The bright pinks, blues, reds, and greens looked like colorful soldiers lined up and ready for battle. The other walls were adorned with large photos of steel mills and other prominent Youngstown landmarks. The pictures were taken by Taffy herself.

She considered herself somewhat of a shutterbug, and she would spend her Sundays driving around the city looking for interesting things to photograph. She had a small, makeshift darkroom in the apartment above the soda parlor, where she also lived. On Sunday nights, the entire apartment would smell of fixer, and long strips of film filled the bathroom, hanging down like strange tentacles.

Her apartment above the soda shop was meticulously kept and well organized. She had shared the apartment with her father until two years ago, when the cancer that had plagued him finally won the ugly battle.

Taffy had spent the last year and some of her father's life insurance check and inheritance on opening the soda fountain and repairing the three-story building that housed her apartment and the soda shop. The roof needed to be replaced, and much of the wiring was out of date and dangerous.

The building had stood on the busy corner of Turin Street and Pershing Street since 1914. Most of the old Italians in the neighborhood remembered the building as a furniture repair and upholstery shop until after the war, when Taffy's father, Mario, purchased it with money he had saved working as a millwright at Republic Steel.

The Brier Hill neighborhood, like most neighborhoods in the city, was affable, and the Italians who settled the area were highly territorial. The forty square blocks were rich in history and culture and were directly adjacent to Oakland Avenue and the big Republic Steel Plant. Many of the people who lived in Brier Hill worked in one of the many mills that dotted the urban landscape.

Taffy knew most of the stories that floated around the neighborhood. She had overheard her dad talking with the men on the block, and of course there was enough gossip to keep everyone intrigued. Such a tight neighborhood birthed an amazing and interesting cascade of stories.

The Brier Hill area was the safest neighborhood in the city. Crime was a rarity, and everyone knew their neighbor and kept a constant vigil on their block. The freelance criminal element was generally kept at bay due to the influence of the Mancini crime family in the neighborhood. Shysters, con artists, and swindlers learned very quickly not to apply their trades in Brier Hill.

In 1948 Mario Centofanti opened a liquor store that specialized in rare and vintage wines and liquors. When the war ended, it seemed as if everyone was flush with money, and the Brier Hill neighborhood was no exception. His customers dabbled in the finest liquor money could buy, and Mario became a respected and valuable addition to the Brier Hill neighborhood. The liquor shop thrived, and around the holidays, a line stretched down the block.

Mario prospered, and in 1954 he and his wife, Connie, had a baby girl, Taffy. Sadly, the beautiful baby girl was never able to meet her mother. Connie had hemorrhaged badly during childbirth and died shortly after Taffy was born. Heartbroken, Mario took his daughter home and raised her the best that he could.

Because of her Northern Italian lineage, Taffy was born with jet-black hair, light skin, and amazingly beautiful blue eyes. By the time she was a teenager, she was tall and striking. She carried an air of confidence that seemed to leave people slightly intimidated by her beauty and fun-loving personality. When she reached adulthood, she was thin with bumped hips and a curvy top. That, along with her jet-black hair, tall stature, and huge blue eyes, was a lethal combination.

Her father would tease her, saying he named her Taffy because he knew she would stretch. She would giggle at this joke, no matter how many times her father told it.

She grew up listening to the Cleveland Indians on the radio and playing stickball on the streets of Brier Hill. Her first job was sweeping the floors in her dad's store, but her main chore was fixing her father's dinner at night. She became an amazing cook and doted over her father endlessly. She played basketball in school and was a talented artist. Fluent in Italian and Spanish, she made the honor roll every year. Mario beamed with pride over his Taffy girl.

As the 1960s began, she would often sit cross-legged on her bed and look out her bedroom window at the street below. From the living room, she could hear the television playing baseball games while her father yelled in Italian at the ballplayers. Directly across from her father's store and their little apartment was LaVilla Pizzeria, an establishment that was entrenched in the neighborhood for both its reputation as a mafia hangout and its amazing Italian food. As a little girl, Taffy would watch the men come and go in their fancy cars, almost always with a pretty girl on their arms. She would watch the men walk down the sidewalk and speak to each other with their hands covering their mouths. They always seemed to be looking around to make sure no one could hear their secret conversations. Sometimes she would see them exchange envelopes while kissing each other on the cheek. On one occasion, a fat man clumsily spilled the contents of the envelope onto the sidewalk. Taffy stared in wide-eyed disbelief at the twenty-dollar bills cascading and blowing down the sidewalk. She giggled watching the fat man comically chase after the money.

At twelve years old, her father warned her that she was never to talk to the boys that hung out at the pizzeria.

"Taffy, those boys … they all troublemakers. You stay clear of them, Taffy girl," Mario said in his thick Italian accent as they walked down the sidewalk in front of their apartment.

"Si, Papa," Taffy said sheepishly, looking down at her feet as she walked along.

Her dad stopped, kissed her on the forehead, and said, "Ora vai a ripulirti per cena."

Taffy nodded and ran ahead of her dad into the apartment to start dinner.

Her childhood was happy and uncomplicated. She never left the Brier Hill neighborhood until she was thirteen when she took the train to Pittsburgh to attend summer camp. Up until then, the entire world was her neighborhood in Brier Hill, and that's just the way she liked it.

With the repairs all finished and the soda shop slated to open in just a few days, Taffy was giddy, constantly skipping around with a smile on her face. She still had plenty of work to do before the grand opening, but her confidence was high that she would be ready.

She spent the previous day putting flyers all over the neighborhood announcing the grand opening in just days. Almost all the forty-square-block neighborhood knew the soda shop was opening, and everyone Taffy spoke with had promised to come by and try one of her soon-to-be famous ice cream sodas.

To work in the shop with her, she had hired three girls from the neighborhood that she knew. Her best friend was one of her girls, Maria DeSanto (whom everyone called Moe, including Taffy). They all came from respectable families and were trustworthy and hardworking. Knowing they looked gorgeous, she had purchased for them adorable T-shirts and hats with embroidered ice-cream cones on them.

The next morning, Riverbend Foods was delivering the staple goods, and she had a jukebox being delivered tomorrow as well. Later in the day, all the linens would be arriving.

Taffy grabbed her bucket of soapy water and started washing the window ledge. Her big blue eyes looked up and watched the pizzeria across the street. She smiled crookedly when a candy-apple–red GTO pulled up to the curb and gunned the engine twice. A young man jumped out and looked around. He was tall and thin with black shaggy hair—a typical good-looking Italian kid from the neighborhood. She stared as his muscles flexed in the tight black T-shirt while feeling the slightest tingle between her legs. She raised her eyebrows and bit her lip.

She knew him from the neighborhood and school but had never actually met him. He worked at the pizzeria and had for what seemed like forever. She knew his name was Benito Squitteri, and his friends sometimes called him Squit or just Benny. She smiled as she watched him walk into the pizzeria.

"Hotti potati," she whispered to herself, making slow, soapy circles on the window ledge. Life in Taffy's Brier Hill neighborhood ticked on and on and on.

CHAPTER 2

BENNY

Benny Squitteri sat at the red light on the corner of Glenwood Avenue and St. Louis Streets on the southside of Youngstown. Sitting next to him was Ralph Testa, another soldier in the Mancini crime family and Benny's best friend. The box truck was painted with a phony logistics company that blended in perfectly with the thousands of trucks that traversed Youngstown roads every day.

Benny and Ralph had just picked up a load of stolen home electronics from a fence in Struthers, a small city that bordered Youngstown and was considered a safe haven by the Mancini family. They were able to operate carte blanche in Struthers thanks to the city government and police chief being paid large tributes by the organization. The only condition set forth by the police chief and the mayor was the promise that the Mancinis would operate their trades quietly and with as little public knowledge as possible. The Mancini organization agreed, and boundary lines were drawn.

That arrangement worked fine up until 1970, when a new mayor was elected. Ted Taylor had run on the platform of cleaning up the criminal activities around the city. He campaigned on closing the gambling parlors that lined the small side streets close to Syro Steel, where thousands of men worked and played hard. The iron-tough steel workers gambled at the local parlors, and on the weekends, most of the single men participated in prostitution.

The Mancini family watched the election closely, and when Taylor won the election by a landslide, Carmine Mancini, the head of the Mancini family, called a meeting of his top lieutenants to discuss the options that were on the table.

Two days later, the newly elected mayor was approached outside the Elmton Restaurant in Struthers and offered a thick envelope stuffed with fifty-dollar bills. The implication was quite clear, even to a newly elected mayor.

"What's this?" the new mayor asked incredulously, looking down at the thick envelope.

"That is a little gift of congratulations from your friends, the Mancinis," the man said, shoving the envelope into the mayor's hand.

"No, thank you. Tell your boss I'm not interested," the mayor said, giving back the envelope.

Mayor Taylor then trotted off to his car while waving to a woman who was sweeping the sidewalk across the street.

The man watched carefully and memorized the make and model of the car and the license plate number. Less than a week later, the mayor's car was blown apart by a bomb as he slept comfortably in his warm bed. The following morning, the mayor-elect stood in his driveway with his hands on his hips, surveying the burned-out shell of his Chrysler. The mayor's staff told the local press that a fuel leak somehow ignited the car.

The realization that he easily could have been in the car took hold of him with concrete finality. Ted was a pragmatist who was able to see the big, broad picture. This was a warning that he could not ignore. The following day, the new mayor got a message to Carmine Mancini thanking him for the support during the election and saying that he looked forward to working with him on improving the city of Struthers.

Benny and Ralph continued the drive back to Brier Hill mostly in silence. They had both worked for LaVilla Pizzeria since they were teenagers. Their jobs were secured by their fathers. At first, they swept the floors, made deliveries, and worked the kitchen at the pizzeria. It was a fun time for the teens. LaVilla was an extremely popular and hip place for people to be seen. On the weekends, the sidewalk was busy with people ordering pizza and hanging around talking. The pair both felt lucky to have jobs there.

One Monday night in 1971, the underboss of the Mancini crime family, Lou Santisi, sat alone at the table that looked out over the street. Both Benny and Ralph were working the ovens and only spoke to Lou when spoken to. They knew the underboss had a reputation as a hothead, and neither teenage boy wished to test the man.

Lou waved his beefy hand at Benny and Ralph. "C'mon over here, boys."

Benny and Ralph looked at each other and nervously sat down with the underboss.

"You two …" Lou said as he cut his calzone into bite-size pieces, "you two want to earn a little extra spending money dis weekend?"

Both boys' eyes lit up. "Yes, sir, Mr. Santisi, we sure do," Ralph said, speaking for both of them.

"Friday night after closing, you boys take da truck out back and go to the Lucky Rooster on Wilson Avenue. You know the joint?" Lou said as he ate his calzone, not making eye contact with the boys.

"We know it," Benny said, looking at Ralph, who was nodding his head.

"Around back, you see a couple pallets of boxes. Don't open them; just load 'em into the truck and bring them back here. Lock up the back of the truck and leave the key above the garage door. Make sure nobody sees you put the key there," Lou said, shaking his index finger at them. "Don't talk to no one at the Rooster, and make sure this gets done," he said sternly.

Both boys shook their heads and told the underboss they wouldn't let him down.

"Good boys. Now get back to work."

Ralph and Benny went back to making pizzas, knowing this was the break they had been waiting for to start earning a few extra dollars.

Friday night came, and after the boys had finished mopping the floors and counting the cash drawer, they closed the pizzeria and went out back to the truck. The old Peterbilt rig was parked out back with the keys under the visor.

Five minutes later, the pair headed up Wilson Avenue toward the Lucky Rooster. Ralph turned up the radio as they weaved in and out of traffic.

"You better slow the fuck down, Ralph," Benny said, lighting a cigarette. "You wreck this truck, we're both in trouble."

It was a fifteen-minute drive across Brier Hill and out to the outskirts of downtown. Even with heavy Friday night traffic, it was still an easy drive.

Ralph eased off the gas and turned into the parking lot of the Lucky Rooster. He navigated the truck around back, and just like the boss had said, a small stack of pallets was by the back door.

"There," Benny said, pointing at the back door where the pallets were neatly stacked. "Back in close."

The air brakes hissed, and Ralph cut the engine. Both boys jumped out and trotted to the back of the truck. Ralph threw open the double doors of the truck and locked them into place. The sound of muffled dance music filled the backlot, while female voices could be heard around the front. They began loading boxes into the back of the truck and neatly stacking them. Somewhere in the distance, the rhythmic sound of steel-on-steel clanking could be heard from the mills, along with the constant haunting song of train whistles.

Twenty minutes later the pair pulled into the backlot of LaVilla with the truckload of stolen merchandise.

Benny carefully backed the truck into the loading dock and turned off the engine. They followed the boss's directions to the T and made sure the boxes were stacked neatly and the truck was locked up. They even made sure to sweep off the loading dock when they were done. For their trouble, the boys each got an extra $20 in their pay envelope the following week.

Eight years later, the boys were again running swag across the city, but this time they were receiving far more than $20 for their troubles.

"I got to take a wicked piss," Ralph said as he shouldered open the truck's door.

The pair was back at LaVilla, unloading CB radios and boxes of children's toys from a fence they had connected with in Struthers.

Benny followed Ralph into the back door, where three or four big men began unloading the truck. Benny was chummy with the guys and had a little banter with them.

"I'm going to get a soda. Anyone need one?" he asked the guys.

The men all grunted no and kept unloading the truck, stacking the heavy boxes neatly onto pallets.

Benny walked down the dimly lit hallway to the front of the pizzeria. The shop was dark, so he fumbled his way to the Crush cooler in the front of the store. He pulled out a cherry pop and cracked the cap. Just as he took a swig, his eyes glanced out the front window to the new soda shop across the street. He saw the lights were still on, but the neon sign was off, and he noticed the closed sign hanging on the door.

He watched, pop hanging by his side, as the girl, whom he had never really met, pushed the mop around the front of the shop. He thought her name was Candy, or Taffy, or Soda, or something kind of strange like that. He remembered she was a few years behind him at the Rayan School, from which they both had graduated. He remembered her being bookish and shy. She certainly had grown into herself, he thought, swigging his pop in the dark.

He watched her for a few minutes until she disappeared into the back room of the shop. A few seconds later, the lights went out, and the soda parlor was dark. A quick second later, the lights on the top floor flickered on, and he could see the soft glow of a TV.

He took one last, long belt of his pop and tossed the bottle into the trash. He smiled to himself as he made his way back to the warehouse to help unload the truck. She was a little cutie, for sure.

Benny, like Taffy, spent his entire life in Brier Hill. During school, Benny ran with a different crowd than Taffy. She was more the studious type, while Benny was more social. She had seen him around quite a bit working at the pizzeria across from her apartment, and they had a few mutual friends.

Antonio Squitteri, Benny's dad, was killed in 1965. The murder was unsolved by the Youngstown Police Department, but that doesn't mean justice wasn't served. Antonio was a loyal and valuable soldier for the Mancini family, and when he was murdered, Carmine Mancini himself took a special interest in seeing the killer brought to justice. Two months after the killing, a man hung in the basement of a safe house on the south side of the city. He was beaten badly, and burns were across his chest. He had been brutally castrated with steel shears. The wound was cauterized by a blowtorch. The man wept and called out for people who were not there.

Carmine Mancini stepped down the rickety stairs, flanked by three terrible-looking men. The boss looked the man up and down, looked over to one of the men who was beating the killer, and nodded. Instantly, the man pulled a revolver out, raised it, and promptly put a bullet in the man's skull. Without saying a word, Mancini quickly walked out.

With the loss of his father, Benny was raised by his mother and aunt, who was an old maid. He was well looked after by friends of his father and was working part time at the pizza shop, which allowed the men to keep an eye on him. His mother was strict, and Benny was a good and loyal son. After high school graduation, Benny began working at the pizzeria full time. This was a job he enjoyed endlessly, despite the long hours in front of the ovens.

Benny began his education in the same world in which his father prospered. He would watch the men come and go and take mental notes of who they were and how often they came into the pizzeria. He would listen to the conversations, no matter how mundane and seemingly pointless they were. In short order he learned that when these men talked, they used codes, gestures, and body language to communicate. When he was asked to run a little errand, he never said no.

As the months and years ticked by, Benny was tasked with more and more responsibility. He was a natural leader, and even at a very young age, many of the organization's men respected him. In short order, he had his own little crew of guys—Benny; Ralph; Ralph's little brother, Mickey; and Stony Dechellis. All the boys worked or hung out at the pizzeria, and on Friday nights when the lobby was full and kids were out on the sidewalk, Benny and his crew watched over their little kingdom.

CHAPTER 3

ANGELS AND DEMONS

Father Frank Gallo trotted lightly across the church parking lot to his car sitting in the lot closest to the rectory. Above the parking spot was a small blue sign that read, "Reserved for Father Gallo." This was just one of many small perks given to him in the three years he had been assigned to Our Lady of the Rosary Parish.

The church service had just ended, and he was on pins and needles, bidding the last of the congregation goodbye. His sermon today was on temptation, a subject with which he was becoming more and more acquainted with each passing day. More than once during Mass, he nonchalantly looked toward the back of the church at the clock that hung above the rear door. There were few places to cut corners in Catholicism, so he had no choice but to let the service spin out.

Gently placing the sacred body of Christ on the tongues of his flock, he imagined blood. Blood. Not the blood of Christ, but the blood of a different flock. A flock he left in 1970.

"The body of Christ. Amen. The body of Christ. Amen. The body of Christ. Amen."

"Am I gonna die today, Father Frank? I don't wanna die."

"The body of Christ. Amen."

"I fragged that fuckin' gook. Blew the fucker's head clean off."

"The body of Christ. Amen."

"We raped that little girl in the rice patty. Man, her pussy bled bad, man, it bled bad!"

"The body of Christ." A-fuckin'-men.

His hand shook slightly as the fat widow, Mrs. Tanner, stuck out her yellow, cigarette-stained tongue and waited for the eucharist. Her flowered dress, gigantic bosom, and liberally applied Chanel No. 19 turned his stomach. He secretly wished she would have a heart attack, die, then rejoin her husband again, where she would continue to be his fuckin' problem.

"The body of Christ. Amen."

Our Lady of the Rosary was only a few blocks from where Frank was born and raised. The bell tower and steeple were clearly visible from Frank's house on Lower Watt Street. They stood there tall and proud, like an icon for all to see. The bell would chime every evening at six in a tone that was in stark contrast to the sounds of the steel mills. When the church bell rang, Frankie and his brothers, Petey and Paul, would all race home for dinner.

Just about the time the boys made it home, Frank Sr. would be pulling into the driveway, smeared with dirt and grime. Republic Steel paid the bills, but a hefty price tag came along with it. The mill ruined Frank Sr., and little did he know that the harsh chemicals and steel dust had given him cancer. The ugly disease wouldn't show up for a few years, but the tiny little seed had already been planted deep in his lungs. This seed was certain to grow.

Unlike his brothers and father, Frankie chose a different path in life. His connection with his own spirituality was always something that seemed to pull him into a world where he could help people on a level that was beyond what normal men could do. He was a good boy; just ask his mother. He had a gentle side that few people have. His father had quietly thought that perhaps he was gay, but much to his relief, that idea was crushed when Frank was fifteen years old, and his father found a *Playboy* magazine under his bed. His brothers went to work in the mills, and Frank went to the monastery.

At twenty years old, Frankie bid his family goodbye and boarded the bus bound for Toledo, where he would begin his studies. Frank Sr. and Maria beamed with pride as their oldest child left to become a true child of God. That night, as Frank Sr. and Maria lay in bed, they both prayed for their son. Maria thanked God for giving her such a wonderful, kind, and giving son, while Frank secretly thanked God for keeping his eldest son and namesake out of the fuckin' mills.

At the monastery, Frank excelled and quickly gained a reputation as a cynic in many ways. The elders of the church looked at this with a mild contempt and slight cynicism of their own. He questioned when the elders thought he should listen. He listened when they thought he should question. He spent countless hours at the mirror, rehearsing his sermons and polishing his aura. Practicing every movement and every emotion, he wanted to be the best priest he could possibly be. After all, God was counting on him, and he would not let Him down.

Two years after Frank completed his degree in theology, he went to the bishop and asked permission to join the US Marines. This was not a decision that Father Gallo made in haste. His father had been a marine, and Frank thought this would be an avenue that would satisfy the yearning in his spiritual soul.

Of course, there was one hitch that nearly everyone brought up during the conversation. The war in Vietnam was in high gear and showed no signs of slowing down. Frank would calmly nod and explain that this was one of the reasons he wanted to join; Uncle Sam needed him, and so did God.

With the blessing of the church, Frank joined the marines and was sent to Vietnam. He earned the nickname Father Foxhole, or sometimes Foxhole Frank. He administered the last rites and heard the confessions of the soldiers. He preached from foxholes and jungle trails. He showed no fear; after all, he had God by his side.

The Viet Cong were the enemy, but another demon put its terrifying hooks into Frank. This monster had many names and many victims. Its trail of destruction was long and wide, and it had Frank squarely in its sights.

At first, many of the enemy's friends and sidekicks helped Frank deal with the unimaginable horror of war. They were casual chums that he could talk to and lean on. They didn't judge, and they didn't care about his vices and dirty secrets. Then, on leave in Singapore, Father Frank met his true enemy and his true savior.

The marines discharged Frank a year after he arrived, and he headed back to Youngstown, dragging his demons with him. He bounced from church to church in a mostly enjoyable pattern of work until he finally landed back in the old neighborhood at Our Lady of the Rosary. Frank and his demons settled in nicely, and by this time he had become a master con man and hid his new friends oh so well.

Father Gallo turned his sedan onto Williamson Avenue and drove slowly down the street, hunched over the steering wheel. His eyes darted back and forth like a strange mental tennis match was going on in his head. As soon as he caught sight of a group of young black men sitting on the front porch, he slowed and turned into the driveway.

"Padre!" a slick and slim man who seemed to be covered in a fine layer of baby oil called out to him.

Frank smiled and turned off the car. He had been here many times before. Although the neighborhood was bad, and many of the city police officers avoided the area, Father Gallo felt comfortable. He was protected both by angels ... and by demons.

"Hello, William," Father Gallo said, shouldering the door open.

His smile was bold and somewhat menacing. If not for his priest's uniform, one might be slightly nervous around him. Of course, the white collar and black uniform lent an air of calmness and trust. This was something that he learned to use in his capacity as a clergyman. Trust was the cornerstone on which he thrived and survived.

The pair of mismatched and inharmonious men stood toe to toe and shook hands.

"How are you doin', Father?" Willy asked slyly.

"Well, you know, God has given me another day," he replied, looking around.

"Well, guess you about due, ain't ya?" Willy said, leaning in close.

Gallo nodded and reached deep into his pockets. Willy watched greedily as the priest pulled out a half dozen small envelopes and began tearing each one open. Inside each tithing envelope was a small amount of cash. Together, those small amounts added up to just enough for Father Gallo to get his fix.

Willy smiled as he grabbed the cash. "In the name of the Father, the Son, and the mother fucking Holy Spirit."

The two men touched hands, and a small bag of sweet and delicious white powder made its way from Willy to Frank. The men smiled and parted ways.

"See you soon, Padre," Willy called out.

"Real soon," Father Gallo said, pulling out of the driveway.

A short twenty minutes later, Father Gallo hid himself in the back bedroom of the rectory, doing what he seemed to do best, plunging the needle into the webbing of his toes. He began to cry as the heroin coursed through his veins, and as the drug wormed its way up, Frank let out a small, sad groan.

In his now polluted and dizzy head, he saw God looking at him with disappointment. His stain was unremovable, and God had turned His back on him.

He sloppily quoted Philippians 4:13 as he drifted away: "I can do all this through him who gives me strength."

CHAPTER 4

GOD BLESS TAFFY

Taffy was up before dawn the morning the soda store was set to make its grand opening. She showered, cooked a quick breakfast of oatmeal and blueberries, and bounced down the steps from her upstairs apartment to her store. The night before, she had stayed up late getting everything ready for today. The coolers were stocked, the register had change, and the tables were set up and looked perfect. She had mopped the floors twice and stood behind the counter with her hands on her hips, beaming with pride. She heard her dad's voice whisper in her ear, and she smiled. "Sono molto orgoglioso di ti tesoro."

An hour before the opening, Taffy opened the front door to let the three girls, Kate, Veronica, and Moe, into the store. She greeted each girl with a hug and mentally complimented herself for hiring such cute girls. They quickly got busy behind the counter, straightening out the candy jars and chatting excitedly with each other.

From the minute the doors opened, the soda shop was buzzing with people and chatter. It seemed as if the entire neighborhood showed up to support Taffy. She spent most of the day talking to customers and hugging people while the girls whipped up sodas and ice cream sundaes. Every table was full, and more than once, the line stretched out the door. All three local TV stations showed up to do a story on the young girl who turned her father's liquor store into the cutest little soda shop. She sat with a reporter from the local newspaper and answered questions about being a young businesswoman. The day was a smashing success, and the cash register was stuffed full.

Later that night, exhausted, she crawled into bed and smiled, thinking about her father. She wondered if this was how he felt the day he opened his own business. Probably, she surmised with a little smile.

Her nighttime ritual was not yet complete. She cupped her hands and whispered in the dark:

"Now I lay me down to sleep, I pray to the Lord my soul to keep. God bless my dad and my mom in heaven. Bless my friends and watch over me. Lord, help me make good choices and keep my mind and body strong. Bless my world and everyone that comes into it. Amen."

She quickly drifted into a peaceful sleep. In her dreams she saw ice cream cones.

CHAPTER 5
SAM HAS A SECRET

Mayor Samual L. Blystone shuffled the papers on his desk with a sniff of irritation while glancing up at the gold wall clock in his lavish office. The beautiful clock on the wall, which was plated in 24k gold, was a gift from the head of the steelworkers' union. Sam double-checked the time on his wristwatch and took note that the clock on the wall was off by five minutes.

Just as Sam was getting ready to press the call button on the intercom that connected his office with the lobby, his secretary knocked gently on the door.

"Come on in!" Sam barked.

"Sam, your 4:00 p.m. is here." She said this while winking at him.

Sam nodded and motioned for her to send in his visitor. A small, wiry man stepped in, smiling hugely at the voluptuous secretary. His teeth seemed to be too big for his mouth, and his wire-framed glasses seemed out of place on his tiny, moon-like face. Sam immediately noticed the man's bad comb-over. He was creepy and gave off an air of danger that made Sam instantly uncomfortable. He was holding a large manila folder in his hand.

Sam stood up and reached out to shake the man's hand. "Sam Blystone," he said.

"Ahhh … so you are. My name is Dominic Capetti," he said, shaking the mayor's now sweaty hand.

"We've met before," Dom said nonchalantly. "The Sheet & Tube ribbon cutting in Brier Hill."

"If you say so. You'll have to forgive me for not remembering. Sit down, please," Sam said, smiling.

Dominic sat down and smiled back at the mayor. Sam stared back, emotionless. Finally, after a long moment, Sam cleared his throat and spoke clearly.

"What can I do for you, Mr. Capetti?"

"Well, Mayor Blystone, as you may know, construction is slated to begin in early 1978 on a new bridge that will connect downtown to the Fosterville neighborhood."

Sam nodded patiently.

"Mancini Construction is very interested in securing the contract to build that bridge." Capetti adjusted himself in his seat and continued, "We feel we have the most experience and the best bid for the city."

Sam shrugged with smug confidence. "Feel free to submit a bid to the planning committee."

Capetti brushed the idea away. "That is something that we would like to avoid. All those bids and companies, none of them have the experience that we do."

Sam cleared his throat again. "I'm not really sure what I can do. I think your best bet is to simply submit your bid along with the others, and if you are truly the best company for the job, the committee will see that."

Dominic sighed. He held up the folder he had in his hand for a second, dropped it on Sam's desk, and stood up.

"I have taken up too much of your time, Mr. Mayor. I certainly hope you will look favorably at our proposal."

Sam smirked to himself and stood up, watching the man quickly leave his office. He shook his head from side to side.

"Fuckin' Mancinis," he mumbled under his breath. He took a quick look at the folder on his desk and picked it up.

He opened the manila folder slowly and immediately became numb in his crotch as he stared down at the black-and-white, 8x10 photograph in front of him. The picture showed, in amazing detail, the mayor on his knees with a man's penis in his mouth.

Immediately, Sam's mind flashed back to that night in the Philrose Motel several months ago when he was approached by the young man in the photo. The man, whom Sam remembered as Pat, took him to his room, where Sam proceeded to perform fellatio on him. Somehow, the Mancinis' had pictures of him and this man.

"Fuck," Sam whispered under his breath, feeling slightly faint.

He stared at the photo for a long moment while certain realizations began to take hold and solidify. They had him. In that instant, he knew the game had changed.

The mayor had always managed to fly under the radar of organized crime. He avoided that world as much as he could, focusing his efforts on legitimacy and morality. From time to time, the FBI or the local police would update him on the happenings in the underbelly of Youngstown, and he would nod and tell them to keep up the good fight.

He avoided the usual mob restaurants and hangouts. When he took his family out for dinner, he would choose a palace that he knew had no mob influence. Yes, Sam Blystone belonged to no one, and that was just the way he liked it.

But now things had changed in an instant. He would have to give the Mancinis the bridge contract and who knows what else. That meant he was going to have to make noise and lean on the city council and the planning committee. One way or another, the Mancinis were going to build that bridge.

Minutes later, his private phone rang loudly, startling him out of his haze. He answered the phone and could barely speak. "Hello," he said, dryly.

"Mr. Mayor. This is Dom Capetti," the voice on the other end of the line said.

"How the hell did you get my private number, Capetti?" the mayor coughed angrily.

Dom sighed, ignoring the question. "I almost forgot, Mr. Mayor. Perhaps your wife would be interested in seeing the photos of you fucking your secretary at the Voyager Hotel last week. I think between that and your obsession with men, you'll have quite a bit of explaining to do. Good day, Mr. Mayor."

Later that afternoon, Mayor Blystone drove slowly to his house, where his wife, Joyce, and three children were waiting. He cut through Millcreek Park, hoping to clear his mind and avoid Market Street traffic. The park always seemed to relax him and let his mind settle down after a long day at city hall.

He had been mayor of the great city of Youngstown for the last three years and was the youngest mayor ever elected. At just thirty-five years old, he easily beat his opponent, who was old and frail, and looked exhausted next to the young and vibrant Blystone.

Under his administration, the city's crime rate was down, civic confidence was high, and even the negro sections of the city were somewhat peaceful. Under his administration, he updated the city park system and expanded bus routes. He was able to persuade the city council to open up the purse strings and pour money into projects that would improve the daily lives of residents. A groundbreaking program to encourage bicycling was implemented—the first such program in the nation.

The four massive steel companies that called the Mahoning Valley home were all showing major profits and employing thousands and thousands of Youngstown men under his watch. The income tax dollars rolled into the city's coffers. Times were good in Youngstown in the 1970s, and it seemed as if the good times would never end.

Along with the big bang boom of prosperity came the dark underbelly of Youngstown. Gambling, prostitution, nightclubs, union corruption, car thefts, and a myriad of other illegal activities ran unchecked in the valley. The Mancini family ran things quietly and out of sight and mind of the general population. When an incident involving organized crime made the papers or the local news, it was generally a form of soft entertainment for the citizens of Youngstown. As long as the mobsters killed each other, who really cared? Activities like the bug lottery and prostitution were viewed as harmless vices, especially for the single men who participated in such activities.

Sam had met and done small-time business with the Mancini family on a low and somewhat trivial level once or twice. His legitimate accomplishments overshadowed any hint of mayoral corruption, of which there was very little. He was well aware of the corruption and the mafia family that ran the town, but the FBI had taken over the investigation several years ago, and the local police were simply in place in an advisory capacity. The FBI was aware of the corruption in both the city government and the police force. The Feds were also aware that not much could be done about the corruption other than eliminating the problem at the source—arresting and putting the Mancinis out of operation.

This was, of course, easier said than done. Carmine Mancini and his circle of associates maintained their stranglehold on the city and protected it viciously.

Twenty minutes later, Mayor Blystone pulled into his driveway, where his eleven-year-old-son, Matt, met him with two baseball gloves.

"Dad! Mickey Mantle or Clemente?" he said, excitedly.

Sam put his briefcase down and put on the glove.

"I'll be Mantle," he said, pounding his glove.

A minute later, as he tossed the ball back and forth, he looked at his big, beautiful house with its perfectly kept yard, the brand new cars in the driveway, and his perfectly beautiful wife staring out the picture window smiling, holding their newborn daughter.

CHAPTER 6
IN THE BEGINNING

On the Fourth of July 1910, the train from New York City hissed and stopped suddenly at the B&O Railroad Station in Youngstown. The throngs of people pressed together, moving in unison off the train and spilling into the station. The hundreds of people, mostly immigrants, all had come to Ohio to resettle and find work, and the Mancinis were no exception.

The train had originated in Hell's Kitchen, Manhattan, where Antonio Mancini; his wife, Chiara; and their ten-year-old son, Carmine; had spent the last ten years. Antonio was a railroad laborer with a strong back and solid work ethic. He did not drink, smoke, or partake in gambling. Working in Brooklyn on the Hunters Point Rail project, he overheard two men talking about great opportunities in Youngstown, Ohio. Antonio had never heard of Youngstown, Ohio, but the men spoke of affordable homes, plentiful jobs, and abounding opportunities. After his shift was over, Antonio, for the first time in his life, went into the public library and asked the woman behind the counter for a book of maps. The nice lady pulled a huge book from the shelf and helped Antonio find Youngstown, Ohio.

That night, Antonio went home, kissed Chiara on the cheek, and patted a young Carmine on the head.

"Chiara, e se ti chiedessi di lasciare questo posto? Per lasciare New York City. Cosa vorresti dire?" he asked in a sincere tone that Chirara rarely heard.

She smiled, "Tu sei mio marito, io sono tua moglie. Ti seguirei fino in capo al mondo. Non l'abbiamo ancora trasformata in una casa. Se pensi che ci sia una vita migliore per noi da qualche altra parte, ti ascolterò."

Antonio smiled, and in his broken English, he said, "The men at work, they talk about Youngstown, Ohio. They say there are many opportunities there."

Chiara smiled with wide eyes, "Si. You say, Youngstown?"

Antonio grinned and pointed his finger gently at her. "Why you smiling?"

With excited aspiration, Chirara said, "Antonio, I have people in Youngstown!"

"You do?" He looked puzzled.

"Yes! From Champoluc. They come to New York due anni fa." She said, smiling from ear to ear.

"Now, they are in Youngstown?" he asked, as his excitement grew.

"Si, Youngstown. They both work in the steel mill," she said.

Antonio smiled and hugged her. "OK, we go to Youngstown and leave New York City far behind."

So, in the summer of 1910, the Mancinis boarded the train bound for Youngstown, Ohio.

Antonio was able to get a job fairly quickly in the mill making good money, while Chiara quickly settled into the neighborhood.

Her people were in Brier Hill, and they were able to arrange the rental of a small railroad flat close to Calvin Avenue. Chiara in no time made the small space into a comfortable home for the three of them. Most of the Italians gossiped with raised eyebrows when it came to Chiara. She had a thin waist, ample breasts, and wide hips. Certainly, she could have as many children as she liked, yet she only had one son. Outside of her immediate family, nobody knew that Chiara's womb had been damaged during the birth of her son, Carmine. Her midwife who delivered the child had called a priest with the concern that Chiara would not recover from the birthing ordeal. The priest delivered the last rites in their small tenement apartment in Hell's Kitchen as the newborn child wailed in frustration for the breast.

Through the grace of God, both mother and son recovered, and in short order, both were healthy, but her days of having babies had come to an end. She and Antonio both had hoped for many children, but that was not God's plan.

As Carmine grew, it was clear the boy was a strong, natural leader. In 1917, a neighbor who owned a butcher shop noticed the young Mancini boy and offered him a job. One of Carmine's duties was to collect past due bills that were owed by vendors who bought large amounts of meat for their restaurants and for resale. Carmine immediately realized that if a vendor failed to pay his bill promptly, the bill would probably go unpaid. It occurred to Carmine that even if debtors did not have cash, in most cases they had assets. In Carmine's head, those were better than cash. If a vendor owed fifty dollars to the butcher shop, Carmine would seize jewelry, art, furniture, or anything of value. He wouldn't take fifty dollars' worth of assets; he would take three hundred dollars' worth. He could very easily sell the items around the neighborhood for two hundred dollars and make a huge profit. The vendors that owed the money seemed more than happy to part with anything except cold hard cash.

Carmine was simply going the long way around. Even though he had to go through the slight hassle of reselling the items, the profits he was making were huge. He would give his boss what was owed and pocket the rest. In most cases he was making four or five times what was owed. The son of the man who owned the butcher shop was a thin, squirrely young man with a slight stutter. His name was Dominic Capetti. Dominic was bookish and conniving. He would give Carmine the names of vendors who owed money and manage the cash being brought in.

Dominic and Carmine became friends, and as the months passed, they began expanding their new collection business to other businesses in the neighborhood. Lou Santisi wandered into the back room of the butcher shop on a Saturday afternoon looking for a job. Lou was a big, strapping kid with dark eyes and a mealy mouth. His hands were huge, and it was rumored that he had killed a man for an insult against his younger sister, Maria.

"Are you good with your hands?" Carmine asked quizzically.

Lou bragged. "I can scrap; I boxed in the Metro league in Chicago. Went undefeated."

Carmine nodded and smiled. "Come with me."

The pair walked to the train stop and rode downtown. On Phelps Street was a small boutique restaurant with a snobbish and pompous proprietor named Arther Anderson. Anderson ran his restaurant with an iron fist and tolerated nothing from his staff.

Carmine and Lou walked around the back of the restaurant and into the kitchen from the alley.

"Help you?" The cook said, looking slightly perplexed. He was holding a large pot of boiling spaghetti sauce.

"Where's Arthur Anderson?" Carmine asked.

"Mr. Anderson? Hang on, I'll see if I can find him," the cook said, placing the hot sauce on the stove.

Just then, the meticulously dressed Mr. Anderson stepped into the kitchen.

"Who are you two?" he demanded, his hands on his hips, looking Carmine and Lou up and down.

Before he could say another word, two things happened. Instantly, Carmine pulled out a pistol from his waistband and pointed it at the cook, who froze and threw his hands into the air, while Lou Santisi landed a punch squarely on Arthur Anderson's mouth. Anderson squealed and fell to the floor. Lou then kicked him in the ass and pulled him to his feet.

"Go get your purse and pay the money you owe the butcher shop," Lou said.

Anderson began sobbing and couldn't speak correctly because his two front teeth were on the floor instead of in his mouth.

"That meat wath no goo!" he lisped out, crying.

His hand covered his mouth and blood seeped through his fingers.

Carmine looked at the cook and motioned with the pistol for him to get on his knees and lay on the floor. The pudgy cook immediately did what he was told.

"The money, please," Carmine said, calmly putting the pistol back in his waistband.

"I thaid, tha meat no goo!" he repeated, sniffling and trying to control the stream of blood from his gums.

Carmine looked at Lou and motioned for him to step back. As soon as he did, Carmine grabbed the pot of boiling sauce from the burner and casually threw its contents onto Arthur.

Arthur yelped and fell to the floor and began rolling around, screaming. The cook looked up wide-eyed.

Carmine leaned over the shivering heap of the once arrogant restaurant owner and said, "You have twenty-four hours, or else this will feel like a warm bath."

Lou then gave a final kick to the incapacitated restaurant owner.

The pair walked out the back door and casually made their way back to the streetcar.

"Carmine, you got sauce on my shirt," Lou said, laughing.

Less than a day later, an envelope arrived with the money owed plus interest. Carmine and his little gang were quickly getting a reputation as vicious and ruthless collectors.

As the years drifted by, Carmine, Lou, and Dominic expanded their collecting business and expanded into gambling, loansharking and selling stolen goods, and extortion. The city of Youngstown was exploding in growth and opportunity, and the Mancini family was running parallel right along with it. The steel mills were being built and masses of people were making their way to the Mahoning Valley. The population continued to surge, and Carmine and his crew took advantage of every opportunity that was presented.

By the late 1920s, Carmine had laid the foundation for an empire that would last for decades. He began courting judges and young politicians. He befriended attorneys, and whenever he was asked to help out or do a favor, he gladly vowed to help. When an especially bright kid from Brier Hill was going to Youngstown University, Carmine encouraged him to study law. Of course Carmine would help defray the cost of the law degree. He handed out favors and influence every chance he could. This, of course, was a strategic move that would pay dividends long into the future.

Carmine kept a sharp eye on the Greek and Jewish gangs that were setting up shop on the eastside of Youngstown. He sat down with the heads of the powerful families and attempted to forge some type of agreement and understanding. The Mancinis were not yet powerful enough to take on both of those factions and win. Of course Carmine knew this, and he also knew a friend was more profitable than an enemy. All he needed to do was bide his time and continue to grow his empire. As long as the Jews and Greeks stayed on the eastside and ran their world within, they would have no problem from Carmine. After all, the city was growing at such an amazing rate, there was plenty for all.

In 1931 emissaries were sent to Youngstown to meet with a young Carmine Mancini and Dominic Capetti regarding the new commission that Lucky Luciano was forming to unite all the mafia families around the country. Carmine had no interest in such an alliance, knowing the more hands that were reaching into Youngstown, the less money would find its way into his pocket. His influence and control were unchallenged, and he was determined to keep it that way. Carmine considered such an alliance silly and wasteful. He had no interest in the dealings of Baton Rouge, New York, Chicago, or any other city, so why would they have any interest in his city? The policies of these other cities were in no way relevant to him, as the policies of Youngstown should not concern them.

The families of New York, Chicago, Pittsburgh, and Cleveland were informed that the Mancini family was not interested in participating in this so-called commission. Youngstown would remain separate and independent of all other families. Carmine politely offered any assistance or counsel if asked, but that would be the extent of his involvement.

This arrangement was accepted by the commission with an air of disdain for the tough little city of Youngstown. The return message was one of contempt and amusement. If the little steel city wanted to play ball alone, that would be just fine, but when they need the assistance of the commission, the doors will be closed.

What New York and the other cities failed to realize was the amount of money that the Mancinis were generating. Had they been aware of the large amounts of cash that were being made through the city steel mills, they would certainly have pushed for the Mancinis to join the commission. Carmine, of course, played his cards close to the vest, never giving out too much information. The pragmatic fact was that Carmine and the organization did not need them. What would they gain? A vote on how other cities managed their issues? Such things were no concern of his, and what Mancini's policies were should be no concern of theirs.

Throughout the 1940s Carmine solidified his empire and remained unchallenged. He amassed numerous pieces of property all over the city. Some were simple houses that were used as safe houses and others were commercial buildings in which he placed both phony and legitimate businesses. Through dummy companies, he owned two of the largest buildings downtown. He owned or had a stake in multiple restaurants and even owned competing trucking companies.

By the end of 1949, Carmine was married and had moved to the quiet and secluded suburb of Poland. He went to work daily at LaVilla Pizzeria, an establishment that served as a de facto headquarters for the Mancini crime family. His world was safe, and those in his inner circle were well taken care of.

In 1957, some twenty-five years later, the topic of Carmine refusing to join the commission again reared its ugly head. The Apalachin meeting of the commission was held in upstate New York. Before it was raided by the FBI, Carlo Gambino took the floor and asked the group about the standing of Youngstown, Ohio.

Michael "Mike" Genovese, caporegime of the Pittsburgh organization, spoke first. "Gentlemen, I know you are considering a tax on the Mancini family, but I can tell you with certainty that in the last twenty years, the war chest that Carmine Mancini has built is impressive and impenetrable. I'd like to go on record as saying any tax is not worth the war that they will certainly wage. Let sleepin' dogs lie."

There was a low murmur in the room, and John Scalish, head of the Cleveland organization, stood up and spoke. "I have to agree with Mike. We are both close to Youngstown, which means we are in the path of any war should it come to that. Gentlemen, I can tell you Carmine is a stubborn man, and perhaps Mike is right. Leave it alone."

The room murmured again, and Carlo Gambino stood up and lit a cigarette. "It's been twenty years. Perhaps it's time Carmine

Mancini joins the rest of us. He has operated on his own for far too long."

Genovese and Scalish looked at each other worriedly and shook their heads. Twenty minutes later, the farmhouse was raided by federal agents, but Carlo Gambino had already made the decision, and it was reluctantly agreed upon by the rest of the commission.

When Carmine received the message that the Mancinis were now to pay a tax, along with a back tax to the commission, Carmine simply smiled and called in Dominic Capetti to get a message back to New York. It read: "Pensa a lungo e intensamente a ciò che stai chiedendo. Ti prometto che l'argento che ti riempirà le tasche non vale il sangue che ti costerà."

One advantage of Youngstown being a small city was that the family's influence reached almost every corner of the city. In most cases it was hidden well below the surface, and people did not speak about who they knew or what they knew unless the right people were asking.

In December 1957, Lou Santisi got a call from a friend of his at the English Hotel on Market Street. The man's name was Tommy Underwood. Tommy was the head of maintenance and had known Lou since they were young. Tommy wasn't on the Mancini payroll, but the pair shared a nice friendship. Lou had gotten him out of a drunk driving charge earlier that year, and Tommy felt he owed Lou a debt.

Late that afternoon, Lou walked into the lobby of the hotel and sat with Tommy. The hotel was doing well, bustling with people coming and going.

"How are you, Tom? Everything OK?" he asked.

"Lou, how are you, buddy?" Tommy said, shaking Lou's hand and sitting down next to him.

"I'm well, Tom. Wife and kids are good?" He asked, politely.

"Everything is great. Feeling lucky these days," he said with a smile.

"So, what's up? Do you need something? Something I can do for you?" Lou asked with sincerity.

Tommy looked around the lobby. "Lou, listen, I owe you for that thing, and for the years of friendship." Tommy chuckled and said, "Not to mention the hundreds of dollars I've bummed off of you over the years."

Lou smiled and nodded his head.

"Lou, there are these two guys that are staying here," Tommy said, looking serious.

"Tommy, what are you talking about?" Lou asked, confused.

"Listen, these two guys came in from New York City last night on the train; they checked in late last night. They dressed sharp and had a lot of cash in their pockets when they checked in." Tommy cleared his throat. "Lou, listen, I've got this thing going with another one of the maintenance guys. When we see a guest come in that looks like they may have some dough or something, me and this guy, we hit their room when they're gone and see what we can get. I know it's shitty, but we both need the cash."

Lou nodded with raised eyebrows. "Tommy, you do what you need to do. I'm not your judge."

"I know, Lou, and I appreciate that," Tommy said.

Lou sighed. "I'm still not sure what this has to do with me."

"I was getting to that," Tommy said. "We went into these guys' room when they went out to eat dinner. We went through their bags, you know, to skim some cash, and inside their bags I seen pictures of you, Carmine Mancini, and Dominic Capetti. Also, there were two pistols and a knife. I looked at their return train tickets, and they were from New York."

Lou nodded and looked around. "What else, Tommy?"

"Well, when I seen your picture, I did a little diggin'. I pulled the credit card, and it was under the United Juke Box Inc., in Brooklyn. I called the company in Brooklyn and told them I was with the Yellow Pages, and we were updating our records. I asked who the owner was, and the nice lady told me Carlo Gambino. As soon as I hung up, I called you, Lou."

"Thanks for looking out for me, Tommy," Lou said. "I think you know to keep this to yourself, and don't worry about anything, Tom. I'll take care of everything."

Tommy nodded and shook Lou's hand. "You tell Maria I said hello, and give the kids a hug from me," he said.

Lou walked out into the cold December night and made his way to his car. An hour later he sat in the back room of LaVilla Pizzeria with Dominic and Carmine. He carefully filled them in on what Tommy Underwood had told him.

Carmine spoke, quietly, "I knew sooner or later this would happen with Pittsburgh and Cleveland being so close. The dough from our sports book, loansharking, and narcotics has attracted the attention of our friends there, and in New York. They must be keeping an eye on us. Gambino wants in here for one reason—money. Those hoodlums from New York, they no care about anything else."

"What do you want us to do, Carmine?" Dominic asked.

Carmine brought the men outside into the cold night air. They huddled close, and Carmine gave the men instructions.

The following day, the New York men were followed as they drove past LaVilla Pizzeria, Carmine's home, and the Italian Social Club in which the heads of the Mancini family all belonged.

That night, the men had an early dinner at Salvatore's Restaurant on Gypsy Lane. After the men had finished their dinner, they strolled casually out of the restaurant. The rain had just turned into snow as the men trotted to their car. Halfway across the parking lot, the men stopped, looking around in circles. They turned up the collars on their coats, shielding themselves from the sleet and rain.

The car they had rented had somehow disappeared. They stood in the middle of the lot with nowhere to run, nowhere to hide. Looking around for the car, they didn't notice the Plymouth pull into the lot and slowly drive close to them. From the back window, two gunmen opened fire, shredding the men and scattering pieces of their blood-soaked camel coats across the parking lot.

Back in New York City, Carlo Gambino received a package that contained a copy of the *Youngstown Vindicator*. The headlines screamed: TWO SHOT DEAD ON NORTHSIDE. CONNECTIONS TO NEW YORK CITY. Along with the paper was a very simple note from Carmine Mancini that read, "Non avrai argento, amico mio. Youngstown è chiuso a te e ai tuoi amici."

Carlo Gambino twisted the newspaper in his frail old hands and cursed himself and Carmine Mancini. Had he underestimated the Mancinis? This backwater hillbilly from Ohio had just assassinated two of his best button men. He wondered out loud how Mancini was able to figure out who they were and why they were in Youngstown. After he calmed down, Carlo began to wonder if Carmine Mancini was correct. Is the price of a war with a city so far away worth it? Even with Pittsburgh and Cleveland sitting on the commission, he wasn't sure. He remembered neither city thought it was a good idea; to him this indicated they would not have their hearts in any fight that he waged. On top of this, Gambino had problems of his own in New York. The FBI and Justice Department were closing in; turmoil in the ranks of the Gambinos was growing, and pressure from the other families concerning garbage and the unions was beginning to become worrisome. Did he really have time and energy to devote to a war with the Mancini family all the way in Youngstown, Ohio? Perhaps Cleveland and Pittsburgh were right; let sleeping dogs lie.

One week later, Gambino sent an olive branch to Youngstown, and Carmine reciprocated with a large cash gift to Gambino. It was nowhere near what the back taxes were, but in the end, Gambino was able to save face, if only slightly.

The Mancini family cemented their place in Youngstown during the 1960s. The organization had complete control of the city, the government, and the steel mills. By 1965, Carmine and the organization had managed to infiltrate both Republic Steel and Sheet & Tube. Through dummy corporations, the Mancinis were able to bill the steel mills for maintenance, landscaping, consulting, and a host of other no-show jobs. The payroll department and many of the auditors were on the payroll, and they quickly rubber stamped the phony invoices. Stolen goods were freely sold in the parking lots and lunchrooms of the mills; the security guards were either conveniently absent or in line with the rest of the steel workers looking at the brand-new items in the back of the trucks that lined the parking lots.

When a rogue element decided to set itself up in business,

whether it be Italian, Jewish, Irish, or any other cultural identity, Carmine would violently crush the upstart long before they could get a foothold in anything substantial. The temptation was great given the huge amounts of money that flowed through the city's underbelly of gambling, stolen goods, and a myriad of other illegal activities. Even the most ambitious and clever young criminals figured it was better to work for Carmine Mancini than to be killed by him.

During the 1970s, Carmine faced a new dilemma—publicity. The Mancinis always managed to survive somewhere between urban myth and self-imposed invisibility. But when an enthusiastic reporter published an editorial on Carmine Mancini titled "Does the mafia control Youngstown?" the name Carmine Mancini was on the doorstep of every home in the valley.

The article mostly consisted of innuendos and gossip disguised as fact. The young reporter was unable to get many people to go on record about the alleged gangster. Carmine himself went to work every day at LaVilla Pizzeria and was indeed the registered owner of the business. He was rarely seen outside of Brier Hill, and by all outward appearances, he was just another hard-working businessman. The few people who would speak to the reporter all sang their praises about the generous Mr. Mancini. The reporter largely ignored those people, focusing more on getting as much dirt as he could on the elusive Carmine Mancini.

The reporter was terminated from the *Youngstown Vindicator* shortly after the article was published. Dominic Capetti sat down with Peter Black, who owned the paper, and explained that the article was mostly false and possibly slanderous. Despite the hospitable nature of the meeting, the undertone of cowing seemed to float just below the surface of the conversion.

A month after the article was printed and the reporter was fired, the *Vindicator* published a two-page spread in the society section about Brier Hill and its wonderful residents and culture. Carmine Mancini was mentioned as one of the pillars of the neighborhood and was praised for his philanthropy and generosity toward the city.

The stability remained constant and unchanging in Brier Hill, its residents comfortable and safe under the watch of Carmine and the rest of the family.

If there was a wedding or special birthday, Carmine always sent a card or an envelope with money. These small gestures won him the loyalty of Brier Hill.

Carmine remembered Taffy from when she was a little girl playing stickball in front of the pizzeria. At her father's funeral, Carmine took the hands of the young woman and softly gave his condolences. He made sure Lou Santisi delivered her an envelope full of cash to help with the cost of the funeral. He had no idea that this pretty girl would play such a pivotal role in the world that he worked so hard to build and protect.

CHAPTER 7

LOVE AT FIRST SIGHT

Moe walked into the storage room where Taffy was filling out an order form for next week's delivery from Riverbend Foods.

"Taffy," Moe said as she looked back over her shoulder, "Benny Squitteri and a couple of his friends are out front. They just sat down."

Taffy looked up and panic-smiled. "Really? Benny Squitteri? Did they order?"

Moe smiled. "Calm down, sexy. Yes, yes, and yes."

"Go slow with the order!" Taffy barked and pushed past Moe. She dashed down the long hall to the bathroom that doubled as a utility room for the lower floor. She looked at herself in the mirror and moaned. The single lightbulb did not flatter the natural beauty she had. Her lipstick had faded, and she looked a little tired, so she put herself together the best she could, looked at herself, and smiled.

Out front, Benny, Ralph, and Ralph's little brother, Mickey, sat at the table closest to the window. The guys all ordered sodas and fries. Normally they would have just eaten at the pizzeria, but

Benny had nonchalantly suggested they walk across the street and try the new Soda Shoppe. Ralph and his little brother didn't pick up on the ruse that Benny was playing. He wanted to go see the Centofanti girl more than he wanted a soda and fries. Nevertheless, the guys all nodded and agreed.

Taffy walked out from the back and sidestepped behind the counter. She was surreptitiously looking up to see Benny. Moe walked by, gave her butt a little smack, and giggled while going to check the other tables.

Taffy grabbed her paperwork and sat down at the table in the back. She had a clear view of Benny and his friends and kept her eyes floating between her paperwork and the boys at the front table. She watched Benny closely as he commanded the table without trying. He wasn't saying much, but the other two looked at him constantly for some type of unspoken approval. This was incredibly attractive to her, and she recognized it immediately as a trait that she admired in a man. Her father had the same type of personality: gentle but incredibly strong, understanding but lethal when backed into a corner. Compassionate, yet merciless. She sighed and swooned in her seat.

Moe walked up to the table, and Taffy could see her chatting with the group. Despite being her best friend, Taffy gritted her teeth when Benny laughed at something Moe said. She knew Moe better than anyone. She was her best friend and confidant, but she also knew she was easy and promiscuous. Taffy was amazed at the stories her bestie would spin about getting fucked by Mike Polumbo in the coat room at the Colonial Bar, taking it in her ass, and giving blowjobs in the parking lot of St. Anthony's Hall in Struthers.

Taffy let out a small sigh as Moe put her hand on Ralph's

shoulder and leaned into him. She felt silly and a little guilty thinking Moe would betray her like that. Crisis averted.

Just as Moe was digging her hooks into Ralph, Benny stood up and started walking back toward her. Right away, she thought, *He probably has to use the bathroom.*

She stared relentlessly at him. *Oh God. Oh, God. Oh. God.* She thought as he got closer and closer. She was unable to drop her eyes.

He stopped. Taffy could barely breathe but managed to smile hugely. "Hi there," she said.

"Hey. Uhhh, I'm Benny," he said, smiling.

"I know, Squitteri, right?" she said, nervously tapping her fingers on her knee. "My name is Taffy."

"I know, Centofanti, right?" he said, pointing at her, comically.

"It's Cent-o-fanti, emphasis on the Ts," she said, awkwardly.

Benny nodded and looked around. "I like the place. Looks nice. That's one big ice cream cone." He pointed and raised his eyebrows while looking at the neon ice cream cone. "I meant to come by sooner. I, I, ahhh, work at the pizzeria across the street."

"I know, we also went to school together. You're a few grades older," she said.

He nodded and shuffled his feet. "So, I know this is a little weird, but can I get your number? Maybe we can go out sometime?"

She nearly fell out of her chair. "Sure. That would be great." She pulled out a little piece of paper, jotted down her number, and gave it to him.

Say, do you ever go to Idora Park?" he asked, looking down at her number.

"Idora Park? The amusement park? Sure sometimes. Why?" she asked, grinning despite the urge not to look overly eager.

"Well, maybe we can go Saturday?" he asked.

She nodded her head quickly. "Sure, Benny. That would be fun."

"Can you get people to cover the store?" he asked, looking around.

"Uh-huh," she said dreamily. "It's not a problem."

"OK, then I'll see you Saturday. Pick you up at say, noon?" He said this walking away.

Benny and his boys left a few minutes later, and Moe pulled Taffy back into the storage room.

"Oh, my God, what did he say?" Moe yelled.

Taffy covered her face with both hands and shook her head back and forth.

"Tell me! Tell me, tell me," Moe barked out. "Did he ask you out?"

"Yes!" Taffy bawled.

Both girls jumped up and down, laughing and screaming, while the customers craned their necks to see what all the noise was in the back room.

CHAPTER 8

IDORA PARK AND MR. BIG BEAR

"What the fuck should I wear!?" Taffy screamed and laughed as she tore through her closet.

Moe was sitting on the window ledge looking down onto the street. "How should I know? What do you usually wear to Idora Park?"

"I don't know. It's different. I'm going with Benny, on a date!" Taffy screamed comically from her bedroom.

Moe sighed, jumped down from the ledge and walked into the bedroom. "Well, bells, I guess for sure." Moe said as she sidled up to Taffy in the closet looking for stuff.

"Here!" Moe said with finality, pulling out jeans and a pink top. "This is kinda cute, and it'll show off your big boobs. It says, "I'm just kinda slutty, not a total slut."

"Good one," Taffy said, nervously. "I've never been to Idora Park on a date, and I haven't been fucked in forever."

Moe grinned and bit her lip. "Well, maybe today you can cross both those off your list!"

Taffy just rolled her eyes. "I like him, Moe. I really do. I don't want to ruin it by fucking him behind the Lost River Ride. Ew."

"Then just suck his dick," Moe giggled out.

"Go get fucked, weirdo," she said, taking off her top and putting on the pink one.

The girls had a long and close friendship that started back at Todd Elementary. They remained close and loyal friends throughout high school and into adulthood. Moe was really the only thing she had in her life that was close to family. Sometimes on Sundays, Taffy would go to Moes's parents' house for dinner. Her parents would always send home enough food so Taffy could eat well all week.

Moe understood her and was happy her best friend had met someone she seemed smitten with. Moe, like Taffy, knew about Benny. They both knew he was a member of the Mancini family and an obvious criminal. She saw the same thing that Taffy did. He seemed different than the others, maybe kinder if that was possible. Either way, Taffy was happy, which made Moe happy too.

Right on time Benny pulled up, and Taffy jumped into the car. She waved enthusiastically to Moe as they sped out of Brier Hill and over to Idora Park on the south side of the city.

The entire day was a blast for both of them. They laughed almost nonstop, and on the Lost River Ride, Benny held her hand, making her feel giddy and breathless. They ate ridiculously bad amusement park food and rode every ride in the park, and as they left, Taffy had her hands stuffed with little prizes Benny had won for her. Benny himself was carrying a monstrously huge four-foot teddy bear that he spent $25 winning for Taffy.

It was full dark by the time he dropped her off in front of the Soda Shoppe. There was no awkward or uncomfortable silence between them. Benny leaned over and kissed her on the cheek.

"I had a great time, Taffy," he said.

She giggled despite her efforts not to. "So did I, Benny. Thanks for everything, including Mr. Big Bear."

They both laughed.

"Hey, next Saturday night, are you busy?" Benny asked.

She pounced. "Nope, why?"

"I was thinking we could do something a little fancier than Idora Park. Maybe dinner?" he asked.

She held her breath, resisting the urge to scream "fuck yes" in his face.

"Sure. That would be great," she said, calmly. "Plus, I'll see you around the neighborhood before then, right?"

"Absolutely," he said, smiling. "I'm at the pizzeria a lot; you're always welcome to drop in for a slice."

She hopped out of the car throwing the big bear on her back.

"You need help?" he asked while chuckling at her cuteness.

"Nope, all good," she said, balancing the bear and other goodies. "Call me when you get home?"

"I will. Good night, Taffy," he said.

That night, she lay in bed thinking about Benny and their day. She was falling for him, and she liked it. He was carefree and careful, simultaneously. He was unlike any other man she had ever met. Strong and self-assured. The term "knight in shining armor" kept entering her mind. She slipped away into beautiful, dreamless tranquility as sleep wrapped itself around her. The endless sounds of the steel mills resonated across Brier Hill, rolling up the valley to their unknown destinations.

CHAPTER 9
CHUGGA CHUGGA

Conrail had been a mainstay in the Mahoning Valley for years. The big freight trains along with coal and iron ore trains crisscrossed the Mahoning Valley in a web of tracks that seemed impossible to follow, and logistically head spinning. The man in charge of Conrail in Youngstown was Henry Ackerman.

Henry had been with the company for thirty years, starting out as a track hand when he returned from the Pacific in 1945. His brother, Jerry, had remained in the army and gone to Korea, something that Henry did not want to do. He had seen enough war on Okinawa to last him a lifetime.

Back in 1945, Henry considered the railroad just a stepping stone toward a brighter future. He thought he would stay with the company a year or so, save up a few dollars, then move on to bigger, greener pastures far away from Youngstown, Ohio.

Thirty-some years later, he still woke up every morning, grabbed his lunch pail, and headed down to the Hazelton yard. He had worked his way up from track hand to supervisor and eventually to head of operations for the Youngstown district. This was a position that afforded him a nice living, including two cars, two weeks in Florida every winter, and putting his two daughters through Youngstown University.

Henry had only one vice. He enjoyed gambling. Not that this was unusual; they all participated in the bug, an underground lottery run by organized crime, and, of course, bet on football. But Henry wanted to win, and the only way to do so was to gamble. Even after he lost, he saw it as a little setback, a hiccup on the road to retiring to a little house in Florida.

Henry had been into Benny Squitteri for five grand in college football and basketball. Henry, the forever pragmatist, knew he would never be able to pay off the debt. Fortunately for him, Benny liked him. They had a good relationship, and every week Henry brought Benny an envelope at LaVilla Pizzeria, and the men shook hands. Henry knew he was never getting ahead, not with the vig that Benny was charging him. Then, in an act that was half desperation and half street smarts, he came up with a plan.

The rail cars that passed through Youngstown were often filled with steel and coal, but there were other cars that slowly crept through. They carried a wide variety of items, from gasoline, to lumber, to household goods. Each car could be worth its weight in gold. Henry sat in the tower watching the cars go by slowly and rhythmically; often the trains were cut up, sending cars to different locations throughout the Northeast. Off the main line were dozens of spur lines that led to warehouses and storage tracks. What if he could divert a car onto a warehouse line that happened to be beside a business that Benny ran? Perhaps Benny and his crew could lighten the load slightly.

Dominic Capetti, Benny, and Henry sat down in the back room

of Dom's Barber Shop on the Westside of Youngstown. The old Italian barber asked no questions when the men walked in and headed to the back of the barbershop. The back room had a small table and a little kitchenette. An Italian and an American flag hung on the paneled walls. The Mancinis used the safe room from time to time, knowing it was free of FBI listening devices. As soon as the men closed the door, Benny turned on the radio and turned it up slightly. Carmine Mancini had taught the young Benito many things. One was that the illusion of safety is just that, an illusion.

"I have taken the liberty of filling in … on our new little business." Benny didn't say Dominic's name. Instead he looked at Dominic and nodded at him.

Henry leaned in close and lit a cigar. "I figure we can skim one hundred tank cars a week. Now, if we can pull fifty gallons a car, that's just a single barrel, no big deal. Shit, no one is even going to miss it. If we spread it out over different cars and use different trains, we'll be more than fine. I can stop and hold the trains for any number of reasons, and nobody is going to ask questions.

Henry continued. "Benny says he has a warehouse off Waverly Street down by Salt Springs Road that's secluded. It has a spur line that is big enough to take in a couple cars at a time. There's also an offshoot line where we can put a few tankers of our own to store the gas. In a couple of months, our tank car will be full, and we can start loading trucks and selling it at a cut rate to stations around the city.

Benny looked at Dom and said, "That's just the beginning. Those boxcars are full of all kinds of stuff we can use. Household goods, electronics, shit, the list is endless. All we need to do is skim those cars a little bit, and in no time we'll be flush."

Both Henry and Benny looked at Dominic. Dom didn't speak, he just gave a little nod of encouragement.

"I don't think anyone will be the wiser. The guys moving the cars onto that spur line won't ask questions; they'll think it's just new track storage. You guys unload the cars at night, and I'll get them moving in the morning. As long as the cars don't sit for more than twenty-four hours, they won't fall out of sync," Henry said excitedly. "We'll be golden."

Benny spoke up. "The boxcars, we just take a few pieces from each car. By the time they get to their destination, which could be anywhere, they'll have no idea what happened. Even if they figure out that they're being skimmed, it could have happened anywhere along the line."

Dominic leaned back in his chair. "And for this amazing new venture, what is it that you want, Mr. Ackerman?"

Henry took a deep breath and spoke firmly. "My gambling debt cleared. Right here, right now. I'll take care of the logistics of the railcars and handle the railroad commission should it come to that. For that, I want 20 percent."

Benny spoke up, "Henry, 20 percent? That's a little steep, isn't it?"

Henry spoke up feeling he had little to lose. "We are both sharing the risk but not the profits. I am willing to make that sacrifice. I am not too far from retirement, and this is what I need to secure my future."

In the end, Dominic agreed to the terms set forth by Henry. If what Benny and this Ackerman man were selling was true, the money would be staggeringly huge. There was much work to be done on the part of Benny. He already had the warehouse and the rail line, but he needed to secure the tanker trucks to haul gas, secure the stations to buy the fuel, find men who could pose as delivery drivers who could handle delivering gasoline, and find good, dependable men to work the warehouse. Benny wasn't too worried. He could bring in Ralph and a few other guys to run the operation and fill in the blanks with lesser men.

This new railroad scam, coupled with the other rackets that Benny was running, was making him a rich young man.

CHAPTER 10

SATURDAY NIGHT IN THE CITY

Benny jumped out of the shower and shook his shaggy hair back and forth. Led Zeppelin blasted away on the radio as he dressed in his best casual attire. He brushed his teeth, grabbed his keys, and headed out to pick up Taffy for their date. It was a quick drive over to Brier Hill, a drive he made almost every day on his way to LaVilla Pizzeria. Benny himself lived just outside Brier Hill right off Belmont Avenue. He had a huge loft-style apartment on the top floor of a warehouse that was owned by the Mancini family. Below the loft, on the first floor, was a flower wholesale company and a moving company. Both those businesses were the nine to five type, so they really didn't interfere or bother with Benny.

He kept his sanctuary surprisingly clean and organized. The loft was close to four thousand square feet and had a magnificent view of downtown Youngstown from both the living area and the bedroom. The single bedroom and bathroom were in the back of the building, while the front was a huge and open area with hardwood floors and massive windows. In the center of the loft was a wrap-around couch and a huge RCA floor TV. In the far corner of the space was a pool table with purple felt and a huge oak bar with seven bar stools. When he opened his castle up to friends, they were always awestruck by the grandness of the space. He had several sculptures and paintings hanging on the walls, and in the corners were massive pillars that sat in perfect contrast to the light oak hardwood floors.

His bedroom had a king-sized bed placed in the middle of the room. The wall looking out southwest had floor to ceiling windows that spanned the neighborhood below. On the far wall was a massive built-in chest of drawers that had pull-out cubbies. The walls were empty and plain; the industrial brick and mortar was a decoration of its own. A huge ghost sign measuring eight by fourteen feet on the front wall read, "We can. We will. We must!" This was a leftover from World War II when the warehouse built specialized parts for the P-38 Lightning.

Along the top of the walls, rows of industrial lights gave off a small and steady glow that in the evening warmed the loft and made the space feel incredibly close and comfortable despite its enormous size.

From a side door just off the kitchen, Benny could go down a long flight of stairs and into a garage where he kept his car. The garage was mostly empty other than his ride, a few boxes, and a workbench where he kept all his tools. The car, a candy apple red 1968 GTO, was bought a year ago with cash. He saved up the money from the pizzeria and listened to his boss, Carmine Mancini, when he said, "Benny … If you no buy it cash, you no buy it at all." Good advice. He tore out of the garage, tires squealing, off to Brier Hill to pick up his crush, Taffy.

At the same time Benny was showering, Taffy was running frantically around her apartment above the soda shoppe. She had several outfits laid out on the bed and was dashing from the bathroom to her bedroom. Each time she would throw an outfit on, then run to the full-length mirror in the bathroom and look at herself, turning in half circles. She finally settled on a cute one-piece black dress with flared long sheer sleeves. She picked out a matching black bra and panty set, stockings, and garters. With a deep sigh, she held up the garters and thought quickly that she needed to buy sexier underwear. Just before she went down to the street to wait for Benny, she sprayed a little perfume on her neck, then after a brief second, she shrugged, lifted her dress, and gave a quick spritz of perfume on her thighs and the small, satin patch that covered her vagina. She smiled and walked down to the street to wait for Benny.

It was Saturday night. Saturday night was always the best night for Father Gallo. After confession in the morning, he had a few churchly duties to perform, but the evening and the night were his. After a solitary dinner of leftover fish, he changed into jeans and a T-shirt and left the rectory. Before leaving, he opened the top drawer of his nightstand and ran his fingers along the syringe and little bag of white powder. This was for later; this he would need later.

After an agonizingly restless drive, he was at a nondescript house on the north side of town. Of course, he had been here before. Like Willy's house on the south side, this was a place where a man of God did not belong. The sin was beyond comprehension, but Father Frank, like the other men in the house, had a disease that none of them wanted, but none of them wanted cured.

Once inside, Frank slipped the man a small fold of bills and tried to control his breathing. In the foyer of the house, six or seven men were milling around and chatting quietly. They all looked eager, and many of them looked as if they could be just another face in the crowd. They were mill workers, teachers, firemen, and yes, even a priest.

The erection in Frank's pants was growing exponentially, but none of the men milling around the living room seemed to care. A short, pudgy man led Frank by the arm into a back bedroom.

"You got twenty minutes," he said, blankly.

Frank opened the door slowly. The room had a single bed, a floor lamp, and a small table that had a stack of mismatched towels on it. The room smelled like a weird, stomach-turning combination of cum and potpourri. The lamp gave off a dim and dirty yellow glow that hid the stained curtains and carpet.

Sitting on the edge of the bed was a timid girl wearing a long white T-shirt and pink socks. Her eyes were both bloodshot and itchy. Her hair and delicate face had tuckets of dried, or mostly dried, semen. Frank smiled as Marvin Gaye played quietly on the radio.

The girl obediently stared at Frank, expressionless. With a deep breath, God turned His back, and Frank did the unthinkable.

Fifteen minutes later, Frank stood over the girl and buttoned his trousers.

"I'll pray for you, my child," he said, in a sympathetic and compassionate voice.

The girl looked up, wiping Frank's spunk from her face with an old tissue. With a little lisp she whispered condescendingly, "Don't bother, praying for me, mister, but I'll pray for you."

The streetlights splashed off Turin Avenue, and Taffy craned her neck, looking for Benny. With each car that went by, she grew more and more impatient and restless. Then finally, Benny turned the corner and pulled up in front of the Soda Shoppe. He quickly threw the car into park and jumped out.

"Hiya, Taffy!" he said, beaming. "You look great!"

Taffy smiled. "Hi, Benny."

Always the gentleman, Benny opened the door for her and closed it gently. In a quick second they were off to The Jungle Inn for dinner.

Benny tuned the radio down, just a bit. "I hope you're hungry."

"Oh, I can eat. Are we still going to The Jungle Inn?" she asked.

Benny looked right and left as he turned onto Burlington Street. "If The Jungle Inn is OK with you, then we sure are."

Immediately Taffy sat up, smiling. She knew it was a swanky supper club that had a reputation for drawing powerful people. She had also heard it was a hangout for organized crime type people. She gave Benny a quick look feeling a little proud to be with him, even though she knew he hung around a bad group of people. She felt protected and safe. She was on a date with Benny Squitteri. Benny. Squitteri.

"Oh, that's fine. I hear the food is good. Of course, I've never been there," she said, shaking the thought. "And it's quite the contrast from Idora Park."

The valet took Benny's keys and gladly accepted the tip he was given. Almost everyone nodded and smiled at Benny, but very few people actually talked to him. She noticed an air of confidence with him. Just the way he carried himself was impressive, especially for his age. He was only twenty-five years old but seemed much older.

They were immediately seated close to the stage, and the waiter politely handed the pair menus and took their drink order. Rum and Coke for Benny and a Long Island iced tea for Taffy.

Over dinner they chatted endlessly and carelessly about family, friends, and politics. Most of the odd first-date conversation had been disposed of at Idora Park, so the pair spoke a little more personally now.

Benny had a sister, Angel, who went to Youngstown University and was studying nursing. His mom was a homemaker, and when Benny's dad died, she left Brier Hill and moved to the suburb of Poland.

Taffy asked about his father. "What about your dad? What was his story?"

Benny shrugged as he lit his cigarette and took a deep draw. "He worked for the Mancinis. My dad got me my first job at LaVilla when I was fifteen, washing the pizza pans and taking out the garbage, that kinda thing."

Taffy grinned. "I know. I've seen you there a million times. I just never had the courage to talk to you. Hey! Remember the time that snowplow ran into the side of the bank?"

Benny nodded, "Of course I remember. The driver had a heart attack or something, didn't he?"

Taffy raised her eyebrows. "Something like that. Go on, I didn't mean to interrupt."

Benny smiled nostalgically and waved his hand dismissively. "My dad was a good guy. He loved the Cleveland Indians."

"So did my dad. He used to scream at the TV," Taffy remembered.

"I loved taking the train up to Cleveland with my dad to see them play," Benny continued, smiling. "My dad hated the fuckin' Yankees."

"How did he die … if … if you don't mind me be nosy?" Taffy asked, cautiously.

"I'm not sure, to be honest. They found him shot in his car outside a warehouse in Riverbend. The police didn't do much of an investigation even though my mom called the detective in charge just about every day for months." Benny went on, looking solemn. "I think they knew it was pointless. My dad was a mobster, Taffy. You know that, and so did everyone else."

Taffy looked down at her drink, then up to Benny. She leaned into him and whispered into his ear, "You are too, aren't you? You're a mobster?"

Benny looked at her stony-faced, expecting her to look away, but to his surprise she didn't. "I never hide what I am, and I never hide behind what I am, so yes, I am."

Their eyes stayed locked even in an almost desperate attempt to drop them from each other. She was strangely turned on, and she instantly felt the urge to touch herself. In that split second, she wanted him more than anything she had ever wanted in her life. She wanted to feel him inside her. She wanted to taste him in every way.

A little grunt escaped her as she tried to shake the thought, mostly unsuccessfully. She kept her eyes on him as he looked away toward the stage. The Poobah Band was just taking the stage for their second set. Benny took her hand, and they walked onto the dance floor. Taffy could barely breathe, she was so nervous and excited. She put her arms around him as they slowly danced to the band playing a beautiful rendition of "Earth Angel" by The Platters.

The dance floor was crowded with couples, and Taffy was holding back her tears of happiness.

He wasn't good-looking in the traditional way, she surmised, but he had a certain aura about him that seemed to demand both fear and admiration. She thought him incredibly sexy in a slightly feminine kind of way. Her attraction to him was almost impossible to define. Her girlfriends might not get the same vibe from him, but what did it really matter? Her friends would think he's cute, maybe even ... very cute, but to Taffy, something in this man made her swoon. He didn't have a reputation as a player. Taffy remembered he had a few girlfriends that all seemed to be loud and obnoxious. This was not Taffy, by any means, and maybe that was his attraction to her? Somewhere in the back of her mind, floating on that dancefloor, she thought, *I'm going to love the fuck out of him someday.*

The light turned green, and Benny revved his GTO and turned the corner onto Turin Avenue. A quick minute later, they were parked in front of Taffy's place.

"Would you like to come in?" Taffy said, nervously and almost sheepishly. Her heart was beating so loudly in her chest that she comically thought maybe he could hear it.

"Sure," he said, turning off the car.

He walked to her side of the car and opened her door. Hand in hand they went up to her place.

"Oh, I like your digs," he said, looking around at his new surroundings. His hands were stuffed deep into his pockets.

She smiled and leaned against the counter. "You dig my digs?"

"I guess you like dinosaurs?" he said, pointing at a shelf close to the TV that held a dozen little plastic monsters.

Taffy laughed. "Yeah, I admit it, I do. If I see a dinosaur toy, I'll grab it. Silly, right?"

He shrugged. "Not really. Kinda cute, actually."

This was the first time since high school that Taffy had had a boy in her apartment. Of course, her father would not allow it, but during her senior year in high school, right around Christmas break when her dad was working in the store, she and Nicky Vargo had snuck into her bedroom. This was the first boy she kissed, and she remembered him feeling her breasts. Even at sixteen, she was well endowed in that department.

Benny cautiously began walking around the apartment. He looked out the front window to the street below. He could clearly see the pizzeria and the drugstore across the street. He looked beyond the rooftops of the countless houses and could see the huge steel mills and the smoke pouring from the stacks. The view wasn't that different from the one from his own apartment.

She followed him into the living room, went to her high fi, put on a Rolling Stones album on the turntable, and plopped on the couch.

"You like the Stones?" she asked.

"I don't *not* like them," he said, smiling and sitting next to her.

"I had a good time tonight," she said.

Benny nodded his head, slowly. "Me too."

As the Stones sang about getting your rocks off, Benny and Taffy started kissing. Benny made the first move, and she gladly welcomed his mouth to hers. She adjusted herself so that he could easily unbutton her top and get to her breasts. He pulled her clothes off, and she thought quickly how she was glad she had on matching undies.

They stumbled into her bedroom and fell onto the bed and into each other. He was kissing her breasts and working his way down. He could smell the perfume on her thighs, and as he moved her panties to one side, he remembered something Ralph, his best friend, had told him. "Pussy, it's like a drug, man," he says. If such were the case, Benny would gladly accept the high.

Early the next afternoon, Taffy trotted lightly across the street, nonchalantly holding her arm across her chest. She made a comical little mental note to always wear a bra when running across the street. Benny had phoned her an hour ago and asked her to meet him at the pizzeria. She didn't see his GTO in front of the shop yet, but she knew he would be there shortly. She had one of the girls cover her shift for a bit while she sat with Benny.

The little bell rang as she opened the door and looked around. Mitch, the fat pizza cook who worked day shift, was on the phone taking an order. He smiled at her grandly and gave a little wave as he took an order. Taffy waved back and sat down at the table by the window.

Mitch hung up the phone and tore off the order sheet.

"Hey, Taffy girl! What's shaking?" he bellowed.

Taffy smiled back, "Oh, you know … same ol' tale of woe. I'm supposed to meet Benny here."

"You want a slice? Got a za coming out of the oven now," he said, wiping his hands on a towel.

Taffy grinned. "What's on it?"

"Mushrooms and extra cheese," Mitch said, pulling the pie out.

She shrugged. "Sure, make it two."

Just then, Benny pulled up in his GTO and honked the horn twice. Taffy gave a little wave and watched as he slid out of the car and walked in.

"Hey, you," she said, smiling hugely.

Benny nodded at Mitch and sat down across from Taffy.

He took her hands and smiled. "Did you get anything to eat?"

"Couple slices," she said, biting her lip.

Mitch brought out the pizza and two grape pops. He slapped Benny on the back and waddled off back behind the counter.

Taffy took a long sip of soda and looked at Benny. "I had a good time last night," she said, seductively.

"Me too," Benny replied, smiling at her.

"I'm sore as fuck. My pussy aches," she giggled out.

Benny nodded, winking at her. "I guess that's a good thing?"

"It ain't a bad thing," she said, blankly, not dropping her eyes from him.

After the quick moment spun out, Benny leaned in to talk.

"Listen Taf … I really, really like you, but you have to understand … My job, this life …" Benny sighed then pushed on, "I know you know what this is all about. You grew up here, just like me. You know who I am, and what I am going to be."

Taffy's mind drifted back to when she was a little girl. In that instant she heard her daddy's voice. "Taffy, you stay away from those boys …"

She looked out the window at the traffic going by. It didn't matter who he was, or is, or will become. It didn't matter what her daddy would think. She was going to love him, and that wasn't going to change anytime soon. She was falling and falling hard.

Amore folle e profondo.

"Benny, I know who you are," she said, blankly.

Her eyes squinted ever so slightly, giving her a dangerous look that took him by complete surprise. He had seen the look before, but never from a woman, and he would have never expected it from Taffy.

Lo sguardo della fredda morte.

He took a deep breath, "Eat your pizza, sweetie. Mitch makes a mean za."

Taffy gossiped about the neighborhood while Benny smoked cigarettes, watching the people come in and out of the pizzeria. He grunted in mild amusement when she told him about Mrs. Ponessi bouncing a check at the Soda Shoppe. She told him about Petey Faggini asking out one of the girls and how she said yes.

"You know Petey?" she asked.

"Pete? Yeah, he's a good guy, works over at Genetti's Body Shop. He's good at pulling dents."

"He has your seal of approval?" she asked slyly.

Benny nodded, approvingly. "He does."

The next hour was spent chatting and laughing. The pair were pooling and puddling into each other, and with every passing minute the strange attraction seemed to grow stronger and solidify what Taffy and Benny sensed. They had found each other. Their life together in Brier Hill had now started, and neither one knew what strangeness the future would hold.

CHAPTER 11

A LITTLE BUMP IN THE TRACKS

It didn't take long for the first bump to show itself in Benny's railroad operation. After a few weeks of setting things up, Benny finally had all the pieces in place. He had set up a front in the warehouse on Waverly Street with a legitimate business selling pool chemicals and accessories. He hired a small staff and brought in top-of-the-line inventory to fill the shelves. What most of his initial customers were not aware of was that every single piece of merchandise was stolen from trucks heading through the city. He ran an ad in the *Youngstown Vindicator* and set up a legitimate LLC. All this was a complete fugazi, of course. Benny could not have cared less if the store did not sell a single item. The real business of the store took place after hours in the warehouse in the back.

Right from the start, the operation itself was bearing fruit and more than anyone could have hoped for. They were draining gas from the tank cars and filling the single car from Conrail that was slated for scrap. Henry managed to get the old car moved onto the spur line behind the warehouse and label it as "gone to scrap" along with hundreds of other old cars. This car was to be used as the holding tank for the stolen gas. Tankers would fill up from the car and head out into the city delivering the cut-rate gas.

On the first night, Henry pushed two boxcars down the spur line and marked them to be removed the next afternoon. Benny and two hard-looking workers opened the big sliding door and looked inside. Stacked neatly from floor to ceiling were hundreds and hundreds of power saws. Taped in front was the invoice, which read that the destination was Dallas, Texas.

Benny looked at the invoice for a long minute, then called out to one of the workers who were already unloading some of the swag.

"Hey, Get me Dante Guju on the phone. Tell him it's important," Benny barked.

He continued to examine the shipping document, turning it over in his hand and smiling.

"Dante is on the phone! Line one, Benny!" the burly man yelped.

Benny went to the office and closed the door. "Dante, Benny Squitteri. How are you?"

Dante laughed. "Better now that the Pirates are winning."

Benny cut to the chase. "How'd you like to put a little money in your pocket?"

"You got a tip on the ball game tomorrow?" Dante joshed.

"I could use that expert skill you've got," Benny said, solemnly.

Immediately, Dante cut the jokes and was all business. He had done work for the Mancini family in the past and had always had a good relationship with the organization. This was, of course, something he wanted to continue. Dante had a printing shop in Cornersburg that he inherited from his father. Like father like son, they both played the ponies and liked to take the train to

Three Rivers Field to bet on the Pirates. Dante was an expert in forgery and document manipulation. Dante and many other people that the Mancinis had on their payroll allowed the organization to operate in such a safe and profitable fashion.

An hour later, Dante and Benny sat at the Hub coffee shop on Market Street. They both ordered pie and coffee. Dante slowly stirred his coffee while looking around the mostly empty restaurant.

"Have you ever come here during lunch?" he asked Benny.

Benny shook his head and picked at his pie. "Naw, too close to the courthouse for me."

They both smiled as Benny slid a plain manila folder across the table. Dante looked at the folder, then at Benny.

Dante reached into his pocket and took out his reading glasses. The paper was an invoice from the railcar that detailed the specifics of the cargo. Benny thought that if Dante could create a new invoice for each load, adjusting the amount of goods in each car, things might go a lot smoother down the line. It was all about putting as much distance between them and the eventual discovery of the deception.

"Well, what do you think?" Benny asked.

"You want me to make new invoices?" Dante said, looking the invoice up and down.

Benny nodded. "It's possible, right?"

Dante looked up from the paper and lowered his glasses. "Not a problem."

A few days later, an envelope was delivered to the printing shop in Cornersburg containing a huge amount of cash. With this, Dante began changing the invoices as they were brought in to him.

That first bump appeared a month into the operation.

Everything was going smoothly, and the money was starting to roll in, big time. The envelopes to Lou Santisi that were passed up the chain were huge. Benny knew in time they would get even bigger.

Henry was in his office at Hazleton Yards going over paperwork and work schedules when a man named Paul Lasky, a foreman on the line, knocked lightly on the door and opened it.

"Are you busy, boss?" he asked.

"No, no … Come on in," Henry said, politely.

Paul shut the door lightly and sat down. He had a small smile on his face that Henry didn't care for one bit.

"So, what up, Paul?" he asked, somewhat impatiently.

Paul kept up the smile. "I've noticed a few cars being dropped over on a new spur line. You know, the line that runs into Benny Squitteri's new business. You know the one, right?"

Henry sat stoically. He felt his stomach do a little turn, and his palms started to sweat. He kept his poker face, not showing the panic that was building in him.

"What's your point, Paul?" he asked firmly.

Paul shrugged and kept the smile going. "I don't know, just seems a little off to me. Maybe I should call Oshkosh and see if they know what's going on."

He stared at Henry with a look of contempt mixed with childlike triumph.

Henry nodded. "I'm not sure that's a good idea, Paul."

"Maybe it's not, but I do know something ain't quite right, you know," Paul said smugly, with his eyes slightly narrowed.

Henry knew this was trouble. If he called the offices in Oshkosh, they would be finished. Enough merchandise had already been looted to cause a stir. Not to mention he was in bed with the

Mancini family on this. If things came out, he'd be finished in the worst way.

"What do you want, Paul?" Henry said, with firm finality.

"I want twenty-five thousand dollars, cash," Paul began. "I want five hundred dollars every Friday."

Henry looked away, then he stood up and looked Paul in the eyes. "OK, Paul, I think we can work that out. I'll need a few days to get the money together. Is that OK?"

Paul stood up and smiled. "Sure, Henry, no problem."

Paul walked out and headed back to the big tower that overlooked the yard. In his head he was going through the budget and figuring out what he could do with the money. Pay off the house? A new car … maybe a Caddy? Take Angie on a vacation to somewhere fancy, Europe maybe? His step was light, and he had a smile on his face. Who knew it was this easy? All he had to do was pay attention to the boards and watch where the cars were going. Most of the guys paid little to no attention to such things, but Paul did, and it paid off, big time.

As soon as Paul left the office, Henry picked up the phone and pressed for an outside line. He dialed and waited.

"Benny, it's Henry. I need to talk to you right away; we've got a problem."

CHAPTER 12

SECRETS OF A RAILROAD WORKER'S WIFE

Ralph Testa and two men from Benny's crew sat in the van smoking cigarettes and talking about pussy, baseball, pussy, football, and pussy.

"I'll tell you boys something, that chick had the biggest tits I ever seen," Billy said to the other guys.

"Fuck you know," Ralph said, laughing. "You sure you don't mean cock?"

They all howled with laughter, including Billy. The trio sat patiently in the van on the west side of Youngstown waiting for Paul Lasky to leave for work. Ralph had gotten the order from Benny, who had gotten his instructions from Dominic Capetti himself. This Lasky guy was causing problems with the new railroad operation that Benny was running. Dominic had whispered in Ralph's ear the man's name, address, and three simple words: Account past due. Ralph knew what those words meant. He immediately recruited two men to finish the job who were both dangerous and clever.

Moreover, they had been the family assassins for the last three years and had obvious experience and showed no fear.

Ralph at first felt the actions were a little extreme until he understood the amounts of money that were being generated by this new venture. Once someone makes waves in such an operation, no matter how small, that little wave can turn into a tsunami in no time.

"You still fucking that little blonde girl?" Ralph asked.

Just then, Billy pointed to the house. A single dim light turned on in the front window.

"Probably the bathroom. He's up earlier than I thought," Billy said.

The three of them craned to see the light.

"Anytime now," Ralph said. "You guys ready?"

They were.

Across the street from the van, the Lasky house was dark and quiet. In the darkest hours, before the sun turned the city of Youngstown into a sepia painting of iron, steel, and concrete, Angie Lasky slid out of bed as quietly as she could. Down the hall her three children slept, and in her bed lay her husband, Paul. She tiptoed to her dresser and slowly slid open the top drawer. Shuffled toward the back was her nicest lingerie. Reserved for weddings, parties, and sometimes church, the outfit made her feel sexy, vibrant, and young.

At forty-six years old, her best days were behind her, and she felt lucky to have Paul in her life. He was a good man and a good father. He had been working at Conrail for more than twenty years and gave her a good life. Their house on Fernwood Avenue, like the other homes on the Westside, was well kept and meticulously landscaped. Though still owned by the bank, someday soon they would make their final payment, and retiring from the railroad would seem possible.

She slipped out of the bedroom and down the hall, stockings and bra straps dangled from her hand. She took a glance out the window that faced the river and could not yet see the dirty thin line of light appearing in the eastern sky, but in an hour or so it would make its appearance. The smoke from the mills pushed straight up, clear in the moonlight. *No wind this morning*, she thought. *Might be a nice day to do some gardening.*

The bathroom door shut with a tiny click. The bulbs buzzed and snapped. She dressed quickly, brushed her teeth, and fluffed her hair. She was getting turned on, and her crotch felt warm and wet.

Paul never fully understood that she was a self-diagnosed whore. Every day when he left for work, she would wait patiently for five minutes, just enough time for him to get down the street, onto Mahoning Avenue and well on his way to the railyards. She would then run to her bedroom, spread her legs, and climax. Every. Single. Day.

Between dressing the kids, laundry, and keeping the house clean, her mind drifted into twisted and bizarre sexual fantasies that she didn't dare tell Paul. Fantasies of threesomes, lesbian affairs with her friends, and multiple partners at once kept her dreamily occupied. She suspected he had created an illusion of her being perfect and untouched other than by him. This was an illusion that she gladly nurtured in any way that she could despite it being a complete sham.

On a chilly November day when Paul was at work and the kids were at school, she had made an appointment to have the furnace fixed. The good-looking repairman stood in the basement with his hands on his hips looking at the furnace. She slid up behind him and in short order performed fellatio on him. That night she prayed for forgiveness in the bathroom for so long that Paul gently knocked on the door and asked if she was OK.

On another occasion she was at her neighbor Kate's house, and the two of them, tipsy with afternoon wine, kissed. Kate at first pushed her away and embarrassingly apologized for the lapse in self-control. Angie giggled and took another sip of wine. Her buzz had grown exponentially, and Kate's curvy hips and low-cut blouse were too much for her to pass up. It took very little persuasion on Angie's part to break Kate. Two hours later, in ladylike form, Angie walked home thinking another little desire was crossed off her bucket list.

That morning, oh so carefully, she peeked out the bathroom door to make sure the kids were still in their rooms. She tiptoed quickly back down the hall on her toes and shut the bedroom door. With a little snap, the lock was secure. Paul rolled over and pushed up on his elbows.

"Hey. Wow!"

"Shhhhh, the kids," she said. "Do you like this?" she asked, squeezing her breasts.

Paul smiled in the dimly lit room. "Of course."

She was on him in a flash. She climbed on him and maneuvered herself comfortably on top of him. Her orgasm came quickly, as did his. She slowly pulled herself off him and moaned as she puddled on the sheets.

"Damn," she whispered harshly.

No matter. The sheets needed to be washed today anyway. That, along with a few other weekly chores, would occupy most of her day.

"Are you working overtime today?" she whispered while getting dressed.

"Hope not. That prick Ackerman is going to ask, but fuck him," he said quietly.

"Be nice, baby," she said smiling in the dark room.

After a quick breakfast and a long kiss goodbye, Paul walked out of the house and closed the front door quietly. The kids were still asleep, and it was a school day, so he was being extra quiet. It was still dark out as he made his way to his Chevy that was parked in the street. He didn't see the van that was parked across the street. Had he been paying attention, he would have noticed the lack of dew on the windows on the van compared to the rest of the cars on the street.

Just as he opened his car door, a white flash seemed to circle around him. He immediately tasted blood, and his knee felt like it was on fire. The next thing he remembered was lying on the ground. The world was muffled as if his ears were stuffed with cotton and his knee had gone numb. In an instant his hand and fingers exploded in pain. He instinctively tried to cover his head, but his arms and hands were unable to move. The world seemed to be going gray as a new pain across the lower part of his back made everything below his waist feel like fire. His bladder let go as he fell on the cement. What little breath he could muster was snuffed out as the small-caliber bullet ripped through the back of his head.

Inside the van, Ralph sat in the driver's seat smoking a cigarette calmly watching the houses and making sure no cars were coming down the street. There was absolutely no doubt that Paul would change his mind on the tough guy posture he portrayed earlier that week with Henry Ackerman about the railcars. He wanted twenty-five thousand dollars and a weekly allowance. Fuck you, fat chance.

The assassination took less than one minute. Ralph and the two men drove slowly down the street to Mahoning Avenue. They turned left and headed downtown, blending into the hundreds of other cars headed to the mills to start the next shift.

CHAPTER 13
EVERYONE CATCHES THE BUG

In 1974, the state of Ohio implemented its new lottery to great fanfare. State Senator Ronald Motti led the campaign to introduce the lottery to Ohio. He sold the voters on the premise that the proceeds would benefit Ohio schools and seniors. Voters approved state issue 1 by a 2-1 margin, creating the lottery commission. Dominic Capetti and Carmine Mancini chuckled at the odds that were given of winning the lottery.

"These people, they spend money on a million to one shot," Carmine said, flipping the pages of the newspaper. "They think they all become rich. What a scam the state has figured out."

The next day Dominic sat down with Carmine and Lou at a small table in front of LaVilla. The sounds of the traffic and the mills muffled and disguised their conversation.

"This lottery the state is going to run, yes it caters to the hopeful and the naive, but there may be genius in that," Carmine said, leaning into his consigliere. "Maybe we could do better, ey?"

Dominic leaned back in his chair and rubbed his chin. "Carmine, the state is in that game for one reason, money. If they didn't think they could get rich, they wouldn't bother. Even with their huge overhead and start-up costs, clearly they see profit coming. We can do better."

Carmine nodded his head. "Yes. I think so, too. There is much work to do, and we need someone who can handle the responsibility. I was thinking about Felix Gabriele."

"He's a good man. Capable and smart. If anyone can figure out the logistics and prep work, Felix can," Dominic said, approvingly.

Within two months, The Bug Lottery, a moniker that the steel workers gave the game, was up and running. Felix proved to be a genius at organizing and coordinating the hundreds of moving parts of the game. Tickets were sold all over the city with the top sales being at the bars and restaurants that surrounded the steel mills.

Felix had the game structured so that the winning number was chosen by the stock market ending numbers every day. This lent credibility to the game, as those numbers could not be manipulated. The main advantage of the Bug over the state lottery was odds of winning, Even more so was the fact that most people knew someone who had won. No, the jackpots were not as big, but knowing people who won gave the player a realistic sense of hope and excitement. Before long, everyone around the mills played the Bug and the money coming into the Mancini organization was staggering. It even rivaled football and baseball betting, which was a staple for the steel workers in the valley.

The lottery commission was unable to explain the low performance of the games in Youngstown. Youngstown was, after all, a big city with a huge blue-collar population. Statistics told the board that ticket sales should be brisk and the players loyal. That was not the case. The lottery commission sent a publicity team to Youngstown, complete with a large van that sold tickets, gave out T-shirts, and gave out balloons to the kids. On the second day of publicity, the van and its enthusiastic team of college interns rolled into Brier Hill. They stopped at the fire station and set up their tent and spoke with the few people who stopped by. The lottery team was disappointed at the lack of support and disappointing turnouts at their stops.

The second day of their visit, the team of six lottery ambassadors finished their lackluster rounds around the city and returned to the Erie-Wick Hotel on the Northside of Youngstown. They all made their way down to the lounge chatting, laughing, and drinking. Just after last call, their van and all its tchotchkes exploded in a fireball sending scorched T-shirts and keychains in all directions. The next morning a van with State of Ohio plates came, picked up the workers, and drove them back to Columbus. The arson went unsolved, and the lottery ended its publicity push in Youngstown.

It didn't take long for the Greeks and the Jewish gangs to catch on to what the Mancinis and their new lottery were doing. The money that the Mancinis was bringing in was staggering. The Mancini Bug houses in the city were quite literally overflowing with cash. The Bug turned out to be far more successful than anyone could have imagined. The minimum bet for the state lottery was fifty cents, but you could bet as little as a penny with the Bug.

Carmine used his influence in the courts to crush the other gangs. Carmine had most of the judges on his payroll along with the police chief. The chief orchestrated raids of the Greek bars and restaurants that were attempting to mimic the Italians. Raids on the Jewish gambling parlors soon followed. The judges levied huge fines and jail time for the number runners and owners of establishments that sold tickets. In short order, the Greeks and the Jews were out of business.

When Benny took over the Bug operation in Youngstown from a frail and aged Felix Gabriele, the receipts were plentiful. Benny made them even more plentiful. He pushed the outlawed lottery to an entirely new group of people and demographics—housewives and the suburbs.

In 1977 the players of the Bug were mainly hardened steel workers who picked up their tickets at the pubs, barbershops, and newsstands on their way home from work. Benny convinced Lou Santisi to look at the Bug in a new light. Steel workers weren't the only ones who wanted a few extra dollars in their pockets. The wives of the steel workers wanted the same thing along with their friends.

Benny pointed out that not everyone in the valley was a steel worker and many of them were unaware or unsure on how to buy Bug tickets. People who lived in the suburbs and rarely came into the city had no idea they could play. Many of them even thought it was some type of urban legend and scoffed at the idea of an illegal lottery. Benny decided to expand the game from the city to the suburbs where housewives could brag about how they participated in an illegal lottery and how they knew a certain Mancini crime member, or how they caught a glimpse of Lou Santisi, the gangster in the newspapers, who actually smiled and said hello to them at the market. All these things were chic and gave the women something to gloat about at their tea parties.

Of course, there was a lot of groundwork to be laid. Firstly, the small cities that surrounded Youngstown, cities like Poland, Canfield, Boardman, Austintown, and Liberty to mention a few, had to be convinced to play ball with the Mafia. They were not Youngstown; they had their own way of running things. Benny and Lou decided on the strategy of starting with just one city at a time. They didn't want to overload or bite off more than they could chew.

Benny and Lou walked slowly through Tod Homestead Cemetery, speaking softly and ever watchful.

"I think when I finally go, I'd like to be buried here," Lou said, looking around. "All my people are here, you know."

Benny nodded. "I didn't know that."

"Yes. Both my parents, my brother Vito … my grandparents and someday me," Lou said.

"This expansion …" Benny said, covering his mouth as they walked. "It's tricky, but I think it can be done."

Lou grunted. He pointed out a section of the cemetery that sat on a small rise. "There. That's where I want to be buried."

Benny put his arm around Lou. "Are you OK, Lou? You're a young man with many years ahead of you. Good years, Lou … and this expansion will help ensure that you, your children, your grandchildren will be comfortable."

"Ahhhh … I know, Bennito, I know," Lou said. "Maybe not so young anymore, but I've got many tricks left up my sleeve. Listen, these suburbs aren't Youngstown. They have their own way of doing things. The people who live there may not be as receptive as you think. Go slow, Benito. Be smart. Don't make any commitments you can't deliver on."

Lou continued as they walked. "Let's start with Boardman. We already have a few operations there; it's a small step and a good step. A friend of ours is on the city council. His name is Richard Pulaski. He has hinted that the mayor and the police chief both enjoy the finer things in life."

Benny nodded. "I'll set up a meeting. Do we know anyone who can approach to carry the tickets?"

"I have a few people in mind for that," Lou said.

Benny looked at him side-eyed but didn't say anything. He suspected that even though the Bug was now Benny's operation, the underboss would have his hand in it. This didn't really bother Benny as much as it would have bothered others. Benny trusted and loved Lou. They always had a good relationship, and having him in his corner could only benefit him in both the long and short term.

"We'll take a bit of a loss in the beginning, you know," Benny said. "Until things get settled and steady, the envelopes to those pezzonovante will be greater than the incoming cash."

Lou shook his head. "The price of doing business, Benito. In the end, we should be fine. I think once we establish ourselves, things will fall into line nicely."

They continued their slow walk through the rows and rows of headstones making small talk and pointing out interesting headstones.

Lou then continued with business. "I don't want this to interfere with the railroad operation or anything else you've got going. Those things bring in a great deal of money, and it's important that they are not neglected."

Benny sighed. "Lou, you worry too much." They both chuckled, and Benny went on talking. "I have Ralph and his brother, plus a couple other guys keeping things tight. No need to worry, Lou. I'm on top of things."

"I understand there was a bump in the road in the railyards," Lou said.

"There was, but I had Ralph Testa take care of that, too. It's no longer a problem," Benny said, giving Lou's arm a little squeeze.

"OK, Benito. You're a good boy and believe me, once we get your plans off and running, the cash from the Bug will buy our influence from anyone we might need."

Over the next month, Benny and Lou visited city officials in Boardman trying to gain a foothold for the Bug operation. This proved to be much easier than they had first thought. The temptation of easy money along with the slight connotation of violence made the city officials more than receptive to this seemingly harmless vice.

Once the city officials were on board and a single Italian market on Indianola Road was tagged as the seller, the first week of sales turned brisk. Just as Benny had predicted, housewives came in with their dollars sheepishly asking for a ticket. The store owners patiently explained that the winner was determined using the stock market numbers from the day before. Most of the new players didn't really care, they just crossed their fingers and bought tickets. They all smiled big and giggled as they walked out. It quickly became accepted, and when Judy Czuba won, the other housewives doubled their play trying to be the next winner.

Benny kept an eye on the operation, and the few troubles were easily remedied by gentle words or in a few cases, violence. A few months later, Benny gave permission for Patsy's Barber Shop to sell tickets. This almost doubled ticket sales and now Lou was talking about moving into Canfield. Things were on the rise for young Benny Squitteri.

CHAPTER 14
STICKBALL

Taffy, Moe, and a few of the other girls from the neighborhood were sitting out front of the Soda Shoppe on lawn chairs Taffy brought out of her apartment. In the street Benny and the guys were playing stickball, and the hoots, taunts, insults, and laughter were floating in circles between buildings. The sidewalks were full of spectators watching the game as the chatter from the players went on and on.

"Vai Benny! Ti amo piccola!" Taffy shouted out after Benny hit a single.

Benny waved and smiled from first base. "Quella era per te! La prossima volta farò un fuoricampo!"

Taffy giggled and leaned against Moe. "That's my boy," she said, laughing.

Fat Mitch got up to the plate and swatted a ball that went into the next block. Everyone cheered as he ran the bases and dodged the parked cars.

The Brier Hill neighborhood was one of the last areas in the city that still held onto its protective and isolated culture. Neighborhoods like Cottage Grove, Brownlee Woods, and Buckeye Circle had long since lost any uniqueness and individuality. The civil rights movement of the late 1960s fused black and white neighborhoods together, but not Brier Hill. Much of this was a result of the Mancini family owning or operating so many of the neighborhood businesses. There were no national chains in Brier Hill. No McDonald's, no Burger Chef, or even a Howard Johnson's. These companies were unable to get permits or licenses to operate thanks to Carmine Mancini's stranglehold on the city council and the zoning committee. Most of the families that lived in Brier Hill had been there for generations, and like the rest of the city, most of them were tough as nails steel workers. They didn't care to have the intrusion of such businesses in their backyard.

The gossip was ebbing and flowing and had been since the turn of the century in Brier Hill. As the guys played stickball, the women up and down the block dished about Donna Pakalas's pregnant daughter, who was unmarried to boot. How Annie Marinelli's daughter wanted to join the army and how she slapped her mother when she was told no, or how Patrick O'Malley drank away the mortgage on the family home.

Even the young girls got into it. Moe turned to a smiling and clapping Taffy.

"You're turning into royalty around here, Taffy. You know, Benny Squitteri's chic and all."

Taffy blushed. "Not hardly, besides … Taffy looked around and said, "You're the one sucking Ralph Testa's dick, aren't you?"

Both girls yelped and laughed. Moe leaned in and whispered. "Gimme a few more days, and I'll be fucking him."

Taffy spit out her soda, laughing. "I can't believe you haven't already! Girl, you need to get on that."

"I'm trying to! I get so horny after I give him head," Moe said, waving to Ralph, who was getting ready to bat.

Taffy laughed. "Well, you keep trying."

The endless circle of Brier Hill went on and on.

Later that evening, Benny and Taffy sat on the roof of Taffy's building. They sat on the ledge and looked out over Brier Hill and the rest of Youngstown. The dirty sun was just setting, reflecting sepia light off the countless buildings. As far as the pair could see, there were steel mills, railroad tracks, and endless rooftops. As usual, the constant metal- on-metal noise permeated the valley.

"Think you'll ever get out of here? *We'll* get out of here?" Taffy asked while dreamily looking out over the city.

"And go where?" Benny answered.

Taffy shrugged. "I don't know, maybe anywhere but here?"

"This is our home, Taffy. This is where we live. This is us. I don't know about you, but this is all I know," he said.

"You know I've only been out of the city once. When I was thirteen, I went to camp somewhere near Pittsburgh. The rivers were clean, and the air smelled, I don't know, kinda nice. I got to go fishing, and we learned about nature and stuff."

Taffy continued. "You know how sometimes you blow your nose, and your snot is brown and dirty?"

Benny nodded.

"Wouldn't it be nice not to see that in your tissue? To live in a place that didn't smell like steel. A place that had some color in it instead of this sepia world we live in. Maybe instead of hearing the mills all the time, we'd hear birds and waterfalls. Maybe the sound of a lawnmower."

Benny smiled. "You never pushed a lawnmower in your life."

Taffy shrugged. "I know, but cutting grass is probably better than working in that fuckin' mill."

Benny nodded quietly.

"I don't know, I guess a girl can dream, right?" she asked, snuggling up to him.

That night, after love, Taffy slipped off to sleep, and Benny got up and looked out the window that faced downtown. The glow of the mill's hot steel made balls of light that lined the river as far as he could see. He sighed, thinking about what Taffy had said about getting out. He had taken an oath, and maybe that didn't mean much to some people, but to Benny, it was an indication of a man's character and a responsibility to tradition and honor. He made the commitment to put this thing he was in ahead of family, ahead of children, and ahead of his wife. That was all easy to swallow before Taffy came into his world. He looked over his shoulder to the bedroom where she lay sleeping and sighed.

Carmine Mancini avenged his father's death. He had made Benny a rich man. Benny was far better off than people might have guessed. While his friends bet on football, drank liquor, and pissed money away at the clubs downtown, Benny saved every extra dime he had. The only vice he allowed himself was his cherry red GTO.

Carmine Mancini was the one who always told him to save his money and taught him to be financially smart.

He remembered Carmine handing him his first paycheck at the pizzeria. "Benito ... You save da money. You be smart with da money, you understand me?"

Young Benny stuffed the check in his back pocket and nodded. "Sì signore, lo farò. Aprirò subito un conto di risparmio."

Carmine nodded approvingly. "You a good boy, Benito. Remember, you always gonna make money, you always gonna spend it. Da trick is, you gotta save more than you spend. Am I right, Benito? Da bums dat play da Bug … they foolish in a lot of ways. Sure, they put da money in our pockets, but they all think they gonna win, when they are all gonna lose. We are da only winners in da game, Benito. Us, not them."

He sighed and returned to his bed. Taffy slid over and encircled him with her arm. "You OK, baby?" she muttered sleepily.

He whispered to her. "Sleep well, sweetie. Ti amo."

CHAPTER 15

HERE'S YOUR BRIDGE

Youngstown city council met twice a month at city hall. During these meetings, they heard and addressed all types of city business. Mayor Blystone, who did not attend every meeting, walked around the chambers before the meeting and started shaking hands and making small talk with the members of the city council and other department heads. This was Sam's strong suit. His ability to charm his colleagues came in handy in the world of Youngstown politics.

Sam nonchalantly shook hands with Eddie Schmidt and moved on to the next person. Eddie smiled and did the same. Being the head of the planning committee and in charge of all city construction projects and issuing building permits and contracts, in theory nothing got built in the city without his rubber stamp. Not even a fence in a residential backyard.

What the attendees in the room did not know was that Eddie and Mayor Blystone had sat in the back office of the Cottonwood Motel out in North Lima a week ago. The motel was twenty miles out of town and through a dummy company was owned by the Mancini family since 1967.

At that meeting, Mayor Blystone in no uncertain terms suggested that Mancini Construction be given the bid for the new bridge. Sam never came right out and said that the Mancinis were pressuring him to get the contract, he also never mentioned that he had spoken with Dominic Capetti and was being forced to use his influence. Instead, Sam used the oldest ploy in the book, money. Eddie was no different than any other public servant in the city making $17,800 a year. Sam explained that he could easily double his yearly salary, and after all, the Mancini bid was reasonable. Two other companies underbid the Mancinis, but Eddie could easily make excuses as to why they were not qualified for the project. In his final report to the city council and the budget committee on why he picked Mancini over the other companies, Eddie cited outdated equipment and lack of diversity in their workforce. The liberal members of the board loved that and quickly signed off on the bid.

That night, Eddie was going to announce the specifics of the new multimillion-dollar contract for the Fosterville Bridge project. His easel had city maps and plans for the bridge, including the road closures that would happen and a timeline for construction. He would also announce the names of the companies that had been awarded construction contracts. These included architects, traffic control, and landscaping companies, to name a few. Of course, the announcement of the construction contract would also be announced. Sam and Eddie were both aware that the winner was Mancini Construction. They had indeed come in with the lowest bid, but both Sam and Eddie knew that the cost overruns would be huge, and of course the city would have to pay those on top of the contract price. Not to mention the high rate of vandalism and theft that would occur and have to be paid by the city's insurance carrier. After all, even with security guards on site, it was in a rough neighborhood, so theft was inevitable.

After the press conference and subsequent glad handing, both Sam and Eddie made their way out of city hall and drove across town in separate cars. The Lucky Rooster was closed on Monday nights, but there were a couple cars in the lot parked close to the back door.

Both men stepped out of their cars and shook hands. "Ed, thanks for coming."

Eddie smiled, and the two walked into the Rooster.

Drinks were on the bar, and music played lightly in the background. Lou Santisi waved them in, smiling.

"Gentleman," he called. "Everything went OK?"

The pair smiled and nodded. Immediately Santisi got down to business. He handed each man an envelope stuffed with cash. "That's just the start. There'll be plenty more where that came from."

The men toasted the city of Youngstown and the taxpayers.

CHAPTER 16

FATHER GALLO'S SECRET PLAN

Every Saturday, like clockwork, hordes of faithful Catholics shamefully walked into Our Lady of the Rosary Church to confess their sins. With heads hung low, rows of old women nervously slid their rosaries in their wrinkled hands, bead to bead to bead. Father Gallo sat in the confessional, counting down the minutes until he could solemnly walk away from the church and get what he needed. Today, just like almost every other day, it was a fine white powder.

He sat in contempt for the faithful, who decided it was best to speak to God through him. Their horribleness seemed to know no bounds, and oftentimes the overwhelming debauchery made his sins look typical of his flock. His mind drifted as he listened to the endless spatter of sin.

"Forgive me Father, for I have sinned."

"I stole from the corner market."

"I cheated on my wife."

"I've been praying for my mom's death."

"I had sex with my cousin."

"I've been taking money from my elderly parents."

Blah. Blah. Fuckin' blah.

The endless dribs and drabs of sin poured out of their mouths like diarrhea. He gave penance in a well-rehearsed and meticulous manner that was characteristic of a priest. Little did they know all he was thinking about was the little baggie of powder and the little pink prize that would be his later that night.

An hour later, he quietly stepped out of the confessional and immediately noticed Carmine Mancini in the back pews. Even in the dark shadows, he was hard to miss with his tall and lanky frame and silver hair slicked back and meticulously kept. He wore a pinstripe suit, and his fedora was next to him. He did not look up to see Father Gallo in the shadows.

The dark corner of the church exploded with light as a man cracked the back door and walked in. He was a dangerous-looking man who wasted no time sitting down next to Don Mancini. The man leaned in close and whispered something in his ear. Mancini nodded several times and whispered something back into the man's ear. This semiverbal tennis match played out as the occasional elderly parishioner walked slowly by.

In an instant, like a strange lightning bolt, it hit him. The men were using his church to conduct their business.

He smiled ever so slightly and thought, *How clever of them. They come here to talk, knowing it's not bugged. Motherfuckers, how about that shit.*

This was obvious to him, even if it wasn't to the spatter of people who were coming and going.

He absentmindedly thought, *It takes a criminal to know a criminal.*

In a flash of desperate and long thought, he surmised and concocted a quick plan to win favor in this world. He was doomed in the next, but for now, that was an entirely different story.

He knew his sins were great, and what if he did get caught? Would he get caught? Probably eventually, and he knew the church could only do so much. He knew some of his fellow priests partook in the same activities as he did, but that was their problem, not his. Certainly, he could have an ace up his sleeve. A bargaining chip, maybe. An insurance policy to ensure that in this life at least, he would be protected.

What if he told the mayor and police chief about the clandestine meetings in his church? He knew both the mayor and the chief on a social level, having hosted them both at church events many times. Mayor Blystone had invited him to play golf on a few occasions, and even though he was not able to attend, the mayor still continued to ask. He may even be welcomed as a hero among the Youngstown elite. The man who broke the Mafia in Youngstown. His head would be held a little higher as he walked slowly through the Our Lady of the Mount Festival while people flocked to him, shaking his hand.

Certainly, they would gladly return the favor one day. The priest is a drug addict. So what? He helped us put away Carmine Mancini. The priest likes to choke twelve-year-old-girls with a bra. So what? He helped us put away Carmine Mancini. The priest steals from the church. So. Fuckin. What.

Father Frank melted into the shadows and disappeared into the catacombs of the church after a long observation. An hour later, the needle pierced the thin skin between his toes, and an entirely new world exploded in front of him. His head spun and twisted itself into a sick knot. The thought of pussy and powder danced as his eyes got heavy. His cock was hard, but his arm was too heavy to grab on to release his fluid. No matter, he thought, drifting away. This weekend would be here soon enough, and soon enough he would be wearing a suit of armor.

CHAPTER 17

FATHER GALLO, SECRET AGENT

His appointment was set for ten in the morning, which was a little earlier than he liked, but he would take whatever he could get. His confidence level was high partly from the treasure of information he had in his pocket and partly from the line of cocaine he did twenty minutes earlier in the parking lot of city hall. Cocaine was not his choice of drug by any means, but when it was available, he would partake. This line was a gift from Willy the drug dealer.

"Here you go, Padre, let this lighten your step. This bump is on ol' Willy."

His footfalls echoed through the hall as he walked toward the mayor's office. Twice he stopped and hurriedly shook hands with a few people that recognized him. He politely said hello even though he did not immediately know who the people were.

He blinked quickly and constantly as if he was pushing the narcotics through his veins. His steps were light and deliberate, like he was walking on water. The door to Mayor Blystone's office grew larger and larger like something out of a cartoon.

Blystone's secretary immediately greeted him when he walked in. Father Gallo noticed her ample breasts right away and tried his best not to stare.

"Good morning, Father. Have a seat, and he'll be right with you."

Almost as soon as he sat, the office door opened, and Mayor Blystone walked out and shook his hand.

"Father Gallo!" he said loudly. "Nice to see you; come in, come in."

The pair went into Sam's office and shut the door. Police Chief Carl Morris stood up from his chair and shook the priest's hand, and all three men sat down.

"So, what do we owe the pleasure?" Sam said, breaking the ice.

Father Gallo, in all his confidence, leaned in and spoke quietly. "I'm not here for small talk or to waste your time, so I'll get to the point, gentlemen. How would you like to bring down the Mancini crime family?" he asked with pure, cocky confidence. The cocaine was doing its job.

Blystone and the police chief looked at each other, eyebrows raised. Blystone shifted in his seat and cleared his throat. "And just how would we do that?"

Father Gallo smiled. "I can give you a way to nail them, lock, stock, and barrel."

"You can?" Chief Morris said, with a hint of skepticism in his voice.

"I can. Gentlemen, I do not wish to have them polluting my church any longer," he said, eyes darting back and forth between the two as he dropped this little hint.

This subtle hint was picked up by both Blystone and Morris.

Immediately they surmised that this had something to do with Mancini and the church.

Morris nodded. "OK, Father Gallo, go on, we're listening."

For the next ten minutes, Father Gallo spun his tale of how the Mafia boss was using Our Lady of the Rosary as a sanctuary to conduct high-level meetings in the church. He embellished the story like a baker adding extra sugar to already sweet cakes and pies. He told of clandestine meetings and secret deals. At points he acted outraged and angry at this intrusive and bold carnage that was poisoning his church. After all, this was a holy place, and such debauchery could not be tolerated.

Father Gallo dabbed his runny nose. "Look, you could easily bug the church and nail them, right? Or …" a lightbulb comically went off above his head, "I could use my charm to get Mancini to make his confession. Who knows what he'll say? You could bug the confessional."

Blystone and Morris looked at each other quizzically. They both seemed to know the priest had gone off the rails a little bit.

"Umm, when was the last time he was in the church? I mean when was the last meeting?" Morris asked.

Father Frank answered enthusiastically, "Saturday! Carmine Mancini himself sat in the back pew with another man, talking."

"Talking?" Morris said.

"Yes! I couldn't hear anything that they were saying, but I can assure you it was a conversation that needed the cover of the church," Gallo blurted out.

"Well, Father, what you've told us is most helpful, and I can assure you we'll take everything you've said under advisement," Morris said, standing up.

They shook hands with the priest and told him they would be in touch.

As soon as Father Gallo walked out, Blystone shut the door and sighed. He reached into his front pocket, pulled out a Winston, and lit it. "You pick up on that? He's high as fuck, isn't he?"

Morris nodded. "I guess that confirms what we all suspected, and, if he told us about what he saw and what his plan is, he'll tell others. Were lucky he came to us and not the FBI. We need to take care of this one way or another. He might grow impatient and go to the feds."

"How close are we to nailing him on the child rape charges?" Blystone asked.

"Hard to say. Months at least," Morris said, looking worried.

"I'll call Dominic Capetti and put this in his court. Let's not fuck around. This is our problem, but it's more Mancini's."

Morris sighed. "OK, Sam. You do what you need to do."

"It's what *we* need to do, Carl."

Sam sat alone in his office absorbing the morning's developments. His mind was traveling in circles looking for a place to land. Perhaps this situation could benefit him? The Mancinis had him by the balls because of that picture. That *fucking* picture. He gritted his teeth and closed his eyes. How could he have been so stupid? This wasn't the first time he asked himself that very question. His entire life was hanging in the balance because he let his darkest urges get the best of him. Why didn't he go home and fuck his wife? She would have let him put it in her ass if he asked. She would have screamed and moaned as it went in, but the kids would be at her mom's, so it didn't matter. If he asked, she would have let him cum on her pretty,

Rotary Club secretary face. But no, he hit his knees and took this stranger in his mouth. Stupid.

This though ... this could be his way out. He paced around his office smoking cigarette after cigarette. Slowly, like a master painter, his work of art was developing. Brush stroke by brush stroke his plan was coming together. If he tipped off the Mancinis that Gallo knew what was going on and told the police to bug the church, Mancini would owe him a favor. He had already secured the bridge contract for them worth millions; now he's doing them another favor. Could he make a deal? Could he trade this information for his life back? He thought so. Carmine Mancini was a reasonable man who knew the value of friendship. After this was over, they would share a happy little secret with each other. One hand washes the other in Youngstown.

Sam sat at his desk and opened the bottom drawer. He pulled out his little phone book and flipped the pages until he came to a name disguised under a set of initials. D.C. 744-2112. He rubbed the bridge of his nose and dialed the number.

CHAPTER 18

PITTSBURGH 4, ATLANTA 2

"Where are we going?" Taffy asked as they blew through downtown and past the endless rows of steel mills.

Benny had a grin on his face. "Don't worry, baby."

"C'mon, Benaroo, Tell me!" She said with her best pouty face.

He looked at her and smiled hugely. "Look in the glovebox."

She bit her lip, smiled, and popped the glovebox. Inside she saw an envelope, inside were two tickets for the Pittsburgh Pirates vs. the Atlanta Braves game.

"Benny! Oh, my God! Benny!" She bounced up and down in her seat laughing. "Benny! Really? Are we really going to go?" She screamed over and over.

"We sure are, baby," he said, turning the car toward the Pennsylvania Turnpike.

Taffy snapped her head, comically. "Oh, my God, Benny! I'm leaving the city! I'm leaving the city!"

"You sure are, baby. Next stop, Three Rivers Stadium."

Taffy began to comically scream while throwing her hands

in the air. Benny pulled her close and squeezed her. "I love you, Taffaroo."

"I love the *fuck* out of you, Benaroo!" she screamed, squeezing him.

Just as they began the drive into Pittsburgh, Taffy looked around comically slack-jawed. She pointed at buildings and bridges while talking endlessly and pointing out things to Benny, who smiled and nodded.

"Look, look, look!" Taffy screamed as the huge stadium came into view.

"Damn, that's huge," Benny remarked, gazing at the stadium.

"Like your dick," she said, absentmindedly leaning out the window.

Benny smiled and in retort said, "Or, your tits."

She looked at him and smiled her sexy smile. Benny parked the car, and they walked into the stadium hand in hand, Taffy skipping along the entire time.

As soon as they got in, Taffy spotted a souvenir stand and ran over. She picked out a Pirates T-shirt and baseball cap and started digging in her pockets for money. Benny grabbed her hand and pulled it away from her pocket. He paid with a hundred-dollar bill, and the nice lady handed Taffy the shirt and cap.

"Thanks, Benny," she said, looking in circles for the bathroom.

She ran into the bathroom and changed into the Pirates shirt, and when she came out empty-handed, Benny looked at her, confused. "Where's your other shirt?"

"Garbage can. Fuck that other shirt; this is my shirt now," she said, triumphantly, while adjusting her new cap.

They walked through the underbelly of the stadium and

emerged into the seating area. Taffy stopped and gasped. The green grass and hugeness of the stadium made her blink her eyes in disbelief.

"Benny, oh my God! Look at this place. Fuck me!" she said, gawking at the advertisement signs and the blue-sky backdrop.

They walked behind the usher to the box seats; Taffy kept bumping into Benny.

"Baby, be careful," he said, laughing.

"Look, Benny!" she said, pointing out to the field. "That's Willie Stargell!"

Benny craned his neck, "Yep, that's Stargell. He's great, and look, there's Ed Ott."

Taffy sat wide-eyed and kept looking from the field to Benny. She leaned over and kissed his cheek as the first pitch was thrown. They screamed the entire game; they drank beers and ate hot dogs. Taffy had two bags of peanuts and an ice cream cone. Willie Stargell hit a home run, and the Pirates won 4-2.

On the drive home, Taffy laid her head on Benny's lap and dozed. Her body was spent, and her feet hurt. The drone of the engine, along with the radio playing softly, was making her sleepy.

"Benny," she said, roughly, her voice hoarse from screaming.

"Yeah, baby?" he answered as he stroked her hair.

"This was the best day of my life; I swear it was," she said, snuggling into his lap.

Benny smiled. "Taf, I love you so much."

"I love you, too," she said.

That night, as she crawled into bed and folded her hands on her chest in the inky black solitude, she whispered, "Dear God, bless me; bless Benny; bless Moe and all my friends. Keep me safe and protect me from those who wish me harm. Help me to make the right decisions and be a strong person. Amen."

In the eerie darkness of the night, peppered by train horns, she smiled and spoke quietly to herself, "Taffy. Squitteri. Mrs. Taffy Squitteri."

CHAPTER 19
LET'S MAKE A DEAL

The Chez Paree lounge in the uptown district of Youngstown had been vacant for more than a year when Charlie Rossi bought the building from the bank and reopened the restaurant. Carmine Mancini himself accompanied Charlie to the bank and spoke to the bank president personally. The down payment for the loan was provided as a gift from Carmine to Charlie, and in short order the loan was approved, and the restaurant and bar opened to great fanfare.

The restaurant catered to the Youngstown elite. Bankers, chairmen of the steel mills, real estate investors, and the like. The first floor had a large restaurant and bar, and the upstairs had a few offices and a storeroom. A banquet room was in the basement where patrons could have business meetings and small wedding receptions. When the Sons of Italy lost their hall in a fire in 1974, the Chez provided the banquet room free of charge for their events until their new hall could be built.

Early on a Thursday morning, Mayor Sam Blystone pulled his wife's sedan slowly into the back parking lot of the restaurant. He had taken the long way and checked his mirrors often to make sure he wasn't being followed. His wife's car was a ruse to prying eyes and to dampen suspicions on why the mayor's car was at The Chez on a Thursday morning. He parked in the side alley between Dumpsters and quickly made his way into the back kitchen door. He didn't look up as he walked casually through the kitchen, ignoring the two busboys smoking by the back door.

Charlie Rossi greeted him at the bar and pointed to a set of back stairs that led to the offices on the second floor. Two dangerous-looking men flanked the bar, obvious bodyguards for the men upstairs. Dominic Capetti and Carmine Mancini were upstairs waiting for him.

Sam stepped in, and both men stood up. Pleasantries were exchanged, and hands were all shook.

All the men sat down, and Sam began. "Thank you for seeing me. I know everyone is busy, but this is important."

Earlier that week, Sam had telephoned Dom Capetti, a man that made Sam's skin crawl, and arranged the meeting on somewhat short notice.

Sam cleared his throat and spoke directly to Carmine Mancini. "Last Saturday afternoon, you were at Our Lady of the Rosary Church. You met several men there. You sat in the back pew and greeted the men one by one."

Carmine sat motionless; Dominic shifted uneasily in his seat.

"You were there for about an hour, give or take. You went to the restroom halfway through the hour."

Carmine continued to stay silent while staring intently at Sam. He slid his chair close to Sam and leaned into him speaking quietly into his ear.

"How you know this?" he said, in a gruff whisper.

Brier Hill

Sam looked at Dominic, who was hushed and still. He cleared his throat and let the men see his cards. Following suit, he leaned into Carmine and talked quietly.

"The priest, Father Frank Gallo, he came to see me with a proposition. He knows you use the church to conduct business, and he knows what it's about."

Sam again cleared his throat and pressed on. "He offered to work with us and have the place bugged."

Carmine shrugged his shoulders and smiled slyly. "Why? Why would he do such a thing?"

"Father Gallo has issues, gentlemen. We've been watching him, and what he does outside of that church is disturbing," Sam explained. "He thinks if we work with him, we'll look the other way on his … indiscretions. Who knows, maybe his next stop will be the FBI and not the local police."

Dominic Capetti spoke up. "Tell us, Mayor Blystone, what are these indiscretions, exactly?"

"He's a drug addict. Heroin and pills. He steals money from the church to support his addiction."

Carmine spoke up. "Who exactly sells a priest drugs?"

Sam nodded his head. "A dealer on Williamson Avenue. His name is Willy. He's been on our radar for quite some time."

Carmine looked over to Dominic and nodded slightly. "Leave the drug dealer alone, Mr. Mayor. We will deal with him."

The mayor agreed and spoke up again. "Father Gallo, ahhh … well … we know he and a group of men molest and rape women. Young women … Children actually, some as young as ten. We are close to breaking up the ring, but you have to understand that we have to follow the law, and sometimes that takes time."

Carmine Mancini gritted his teeth in disgust and said, "Che tipo di animale ferisce i bambini."

The room held its silence for a few seconds until Dominic spoke. "These men, you have their names, too?"

Sam shrugged. "I can give you one; that's all we have for now. Rest assured that when we are able to identify the rest, you'll know. The wheels of justice turn slow, gentlemen. In the outside world, things take time. Sometimes a very long time."

"This is true," Carmine replied. "And sometimes they fail to turn at all."

All three men nodded in agreement.

After a few seconds of thought, Dominic spoke up. "So, Mayor Blystone, you have brought us this information of which we are grateful. What is it that you want in return?"

Sam looked back at Dominic. "The photograph. I want it, and the negative." He then turned to Carmine. "I want your word as a man that you will forget about that incident and never speak of it again."

Carmine stared at Sam; he had a hint of disgust on his face. "This picture. It shows you performing a sex act on a man I understand."

Sam looked away and spoke hastily. "Do we have a deal?"

"I'll get back to you soon, Mr. Blystone. In the meantime, thank you for the information. It's always comforting knowing good friends like you constantly have our best interest at heart."

All the men stood up, and Sam shook hands and left. Carmine shut the door and lit a cigar.

"So, what do you think?" Carmine said, between puffs.

Dominic shrugged. "The priest, we need to fix that along with the others. Willy and the man that shares Father Gallo's lust for children."

Carmine nodded. "Let me ponder this, Dominic. The mayor, if we give him what he wants, we'll have nothing on him. If he chooses to martyr himself for some great cause, our hands are tied. He's already shown us his cards—a foolish move on his part."

Dominic agreed. "Just let me know what you need me to do."

Carmine tapped the ash from his cigar. "The name … that man; get it right away."

Later that day via a courier, an envelope was clandestinely delivered to La Villa Pizzeria through a series of handoffs. Dominic opened it, and inside were two names written in block script. An address was written below each name. At the bottom of the page was the name Willy Smith and the address, 2112 Williamson. Just above it was Chuck Wakowski. 1115 East Avondale. Frank memorized the names and addresses and destroyed the paper. He then picked up the phone and began calling.

CHAPTER 20
A DROP OF ANISETTE

After the meeting with the mayor, Carmine was driven home. He had a modest home in Poland Township that blended seamlessly with the others on the street. His wife, Anette, kept their home spotless and meticulously organized. He kissed her cheek and asked her for a little cup of anisette along with some fresh bomboloni.

The house had a huge screened-in back porch that in the summer was shaded and cool. Carmine enjoyed the wonderful weather and listened to the wind blowing the massive oaks and maples that filled his back yard. With his anisette set by his side, he relaxed as the evening began to take hold of the world.

Today's events consumed most of his thoughts. This Willy man, this drug dealer who sells his poison to a priest, needed to go. The same with this pedophile that preys on children. Blystone had only given them one single name. He made a mental note to have Dominic pressure him into getting all the names.

As for the priest, this may prove to be trickier. The priest was a well-respected and admired man of the cloth. The city of Youngstown would reel from the death of this man not knowing the true nature of the Beast. The police will be under huge pressure to catch the killer, not to mention the FBI might show an interest in this case. It would be tricky, and the fallout will be great. If the church discovers this Father Gallo was a child rapist, they might perhaps want to dispose of this quickly and quietly. If they knew he was also a drug addict, it may really push them to move along even quicker. Carmine had dealings with the Catholic Diocese on a few occasions over the years, and it was evident that they, like his own organization, had its own agenda and cause. *They are not so different from us*, he thought.

Carmine rubbed his temples, letting these thoughts mix in his head. Yes, the killing of Willy and the pedophile were simple cut-and-dry acts. This could be achieved easily and without much of a problem. He would let Lou Santisi figure out the details. Father Gallo was a little different in many ways.

His thoughts carried him back to 1917. This was the year he killed his first man in a fight at the Pyatt Street Fish Market. He didn't use a gun but used his bare hands. This man tried to rob him behind the market. A young Carmine had gone behind an old fish shed to relieve himself, and just as he was buttoning his trousers, an Irish with a small knife came at him demanding his fish and the little money he had in his pocket. Carmine eyed the older man up and down and immediately knew he was quicker, smarter, and more clever than the Irish. Young Carmine easily took the knife and tossed it away. The man came at him in a fit of rage. Carmine swung and connected with the would-be thief, and in a flash he was on top of him and with his forearm choked the life out of him. The man lay still and lifeless. Carmine grabbed his fish and ran down a small hill in the back of the market and onto Wayne

Avenue, constantly looking over his shoulder. From there he caught a streetcar back to Brier Hill.

The cornerstone of Carmine Mancini's empire was loyalty and trust. Without these things, his world and everyone in it would cease to exist. His entire life he had surrounded himself with men who shared his same values and ideals. They obeyed him out of tradition and respect. In some cases, they committed murder for him. This task, the task of murder, was an order that would ensure loyalty, something that was imperative to his world. After much thought, Carmine decided on the assassin to be tasked with killing the priest.

He switched mental gears, recalling the family's association with Mayor Blystone. Carmine had no respect for Sam Blystone and his viciously sinful ways, but the mayor was the new lynchpin for corruption in the city. For a few years, the mayor was able to avoid Carmine and the organization, but that wouldn't last forever. It didn't take them long to figure out the mayor's secrets. Members of Lou Santisi's crew had trailed the mayor and discovered he had a taste for men. When Carmine was told of this he smiled. "Do you suppose his wife is aware of his playfully sinful weekends?"

There was more. The mayor had a curvy and flirty secretary that he would rendezvous with at the Voyager Hotel occasionally. She too was a married, a woman with children.

"Our mayor is quite the playboy, isn't he," Carmine remarked. "Let's let Mayor Blystone know we are aware of his vices."

They had the chief of police and every member of city council in their back pocket, not to mention the prosecutor, the city law director, and the sheriff. They didn't need the mayor, but now they knew they had him, and that was not going to change.

Carmine took a deep breath and sighed. His world felt secure, and everyone in it was well taken care of.

CHAPTER 21

CINDERELLA

"What's it like? You know, being a member of the Mancini family?" she asked in a somewhat reluctantly timid voice.

They sat on the Cinderella Bridge in Millcreek Park, their sneakered feet dangling over the edge, tossing hunks of bread into the stream watching the ducks nibble on the treat. The bridge was a favorite spot of hers. It offered a brief break from the dirty air and the smell of steel that flooded Brier Hill. Millcreek Park was on the other side of town and upwind from the mills. The air here seemed a little fresher when she took a deep breath.

Benny shrugged looking at Taffy.

"It's my job, I guess," he said, hoping the subject would disappear as quickly as it came up.

Taffy pushed on gently, "No, really, Benny. I know you work at the pizzeria, but you're gone a lot, too. I know you're not just zipping around Youngstown in your GTO with Ralph and your boys."

Benny shrugged and smiled. "I run errands for Lou and Dominic, sometimes."

She wasn't buying it. "You don't want to tell me?"

"Nothing much to tell, Taffy." He tossed another hunk of bread into the stream. "I know you're not stupid, are you?"

She leaned into him. "No, Benny, I'm not. Don't forget we grew up in the same neighborhood. I've seen the type of people that come in and out of LaVilla. I've watched them my whole life."

"What do you want me to say, Taffy? That I'm a criminal? OK, so I am. That I sell stolen shit? OK, cool, I guess I do." He looked at her and said, "That's all I know, Taffy. From the time I was just a little kid, I hung out at the pizzeria with my dad."

Taffy smiled, "It's OK, Benny. I know who you are. Have you ever been arrested?"

"He shook his head. "No, that can't really happen to me. Carmine would make sure of it."

"Carmine would make sure of it?" she questioned.

He shrugged. "Yeah, the man has a lot of friends, Taffy. A lot of friends."

They stood up and brushed off their butts. He held her hand as they slowly walked across the bridge toward the parking lot. She stopped, looked around, and gave him a kiss on the cheek.

"I want you to promise me you'll always be careful, Benny Squitteri," she said, smiling.

He shrugged and said, "I promise to always be careful, Taffy Centofanti."

She jumped on his back, and he gave her a piggyback ride all the way to the car. Once there, she pushed him against the car and kissed his mouth deeply. She scanned the parking lot, and it was empty other than a few cars scattered throughout. She took his hand with a mischievous grin, and with her other hand, she easily snapped open her jeans and pulled down her zipper. She then slowly put his hand down the front of her pants.

"Let's go home," she said in choppy little breaths.

CHAPTER 22
THE PRICE OF SIN

"Because your fat ass need exercise!" Shanice barked at Willy as he stormed out of the house, slamming the screen door.

He angrily started the walk up Williamson Avenue to the corner market for a six pack of beer and cigarettes. His bitch was right; he did need some exercise. In high school he could carry a football like no other, but now his body was full of chemicals and fat. After just one block of walking he felt winded and dizzy.

"Fuckin' smack," he mumbled. "Maybe I should take it easy on he-ron."

Willy was only thirty years old and already a veteran of the drug trade that bubbled just below the surface in Youngstown. Almost all his buyers were black and lived in the same neighborhood as Willy, which was, of course, by design. Not only could Willy keep an eye on his customers, but if they ended up owing him money, they were easily found.

Willy had six children, all of whom were now in foster care. Their mothers were junkies and whores that he fucked on a whim, and in his numb-minded state, he pushed his cock into them as deep as he could and let his sperm fill them up. The next morning he barely remembered the girl's name, only the incredible skills she had with her mouth.

He began moving drugs for heavy-hitting dealers when he was just eighteen years old, desperate and unemployed. Back then he had a small sense of responsibility and wanted to do what was right. He would give money, formula, and toys to his children and their no-good whore mothers. In no time, he found out the money was being spent on drugs; the toys and formula were sold before the end of the day.

A bitter, broken, and now casual drug-using Willy broke ties with the whore mothers and began selling drugs around his neighborhood for himself. In short order, Willy had created quite an empire. He kept his business low key and never screwed his suppliers. He paid off the beat cops with huge envelopes of cash and tried to keep the violence to a minimum. He rarely gave credit, and when he did, the vig was small and payments could easily be made. His product was cut generously and never laced with garbage like laxatives. His customers loved him and continued coming back for more.

His footfalls on the sidewalk felt heavy, but for the first time since he could remember, he took note of how nice of a day it was. The sun felt warm and comforting against his black face. He took deliberate deep breaths and looked up at the sparse clouds in the blue sky in semiawe. This was the first time since he was a kid that he noted the clouds and the sky.

"Well, I'll be a motherfucker," he said, smiling as he trotted along Williamson.

The gunshot rang the neighborhood bell. Most people casually glanced out their windows; others simply ignored it. Many knew the sound well, and some, like Bubba Thortan, an old school gang banger, knew it was a 9mm round.

The shot caught Willy in the side of the head, twisting him around in a half circle. A yarmulke-sized skull plate was immediately removed from his body and flung against a fire hydrant. He hit his knees and gasped. His brain was visible and gleaming in the beautiful sun he was admiring just a few seconds earlier. The second shot tore through his shirt and destroyed his heart. He lay face first on the sidewalk with a growing pool of deep red blood running off the sidewalk and into the gutter.

That same afternoon Chuckie Wakowski sat on the park bench, a copy of the *Youngstown Vindicator* on his lap. He scanned the headlines with mild interest as his eyes darted between the paper and the playground. Crandall Park was one of his favorite haunts. He came here almost every day after his job at Republic Steel where he had been a custodian for ten years. It was a steady nine to five job with a pension and vacation pay. His job afforded him the luxury of solitude, something that he treasured. He kept to himself and said little as he cleaned the toilets and mopped the floors in the company cafeteria.

When his shift ended, he would often stop at the corner store and get a paper and a soda pop. His next stop would be Crandall Park, where he would stroll the grounds until he found a nice bench with a view of the children playing ball or, if he were lucky, playing in the fountains.

For a middle-aged man who was both childless and a bachelor, this was somewhat eyebrow-raising behavior. Luckily for Chuck, no one paid him any particular attention as he blended in with the hundreds of other people who enjoyed the park daily. The laughter of children, especially girls, set off an internal trigger somewhere deep inside him—a longing and a pressure that only a small group of people could understand.

The newspaper covered his erection as he watched the young girls playing in the fountain. His mind floated away to a sick and dark place where on Saturday nights he could turn these desires into reality.

Unbeknownst to Chuckie, across the playground were two men slowly circling around the monkey bars, making their way to his side of the big playground. Once there, the two nonchalantly strolled to the parking lot and positioned themselves close to Chuckie's car.

A half hour later, Chuckie walked across the parking lot to his car. His only thought was to get home to his little house where he could lie on his single bed and squirt copious amounts of sperm onto his stomach, fantasizing about fucking one of the little girls on the playground. Before he could get anywhere near his Ford, he felt something digging into his side. It felt like a small pipe or pencil. He was being pushed into a car that had sped up next to them and stopped abruptly. They drove him in silence to a warehouse on the east side of the city that sat on the banks of the Mahoning River. By this time, Chuckie was crying and pleading with the men to let him go.

The following morning, Chuckie's supervisor leaned into the janitor's breakroom. "Anyone seen Chuck Wakowski? He didn't show up today and no call off."

Four days later, the police had a report of an abandoned car that had been in the parking lot of Crandall Park for multiple days.

The car was towed and put into the back of Terlesky's junk yard on Poland Avenue where it would eventually be scrapped.

The bank foreclosed on his modest home, and without Chuckie to contest the foreclosure, the bank took his house by default. His credit cards went unpaid and were eventually closed along with his bank accounts. In a few short years, any trace of Chuckie Wakowski was completely erased other than a mostly rotted corpse tethered to four cinder blocks at the bottom of McKelvey Lake on the east side of the city.

CHAPTER 23

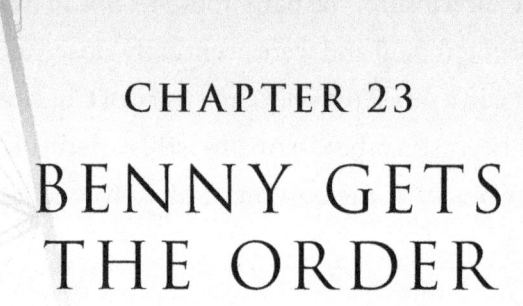

BENNY GETS THE ORDER

In the back of LaVilla was a small office where the Mancini family did some, but not all of its business. Carmine Mancini sat by himself in the office in deep thought. Mancini was not a man who acted rashly or out of emotion. He was a thinker, a logical man whose decisions were calculated and precise.

Mancini drew a deep breath, stood up, and walked to the office door. He leaned out and called to a small, wiry man who was sweeping the floor.

"Is Benito out front?" he asked, lighting his cigar.

The wiry man nodded and walked toward the front of the shop. A second later, Benny walked back wiping his hands on his apron.

"You wanted to see me, Carmine?" Benny asked, politely.

"Benito … Come in," Carmine said in his thick Italian accent. He ushered Benny into the office with his boney hand on Benny's shoulder. He left the office door open, allowing the clatter and bustle of the pizzeria to float in.

They sat down across from each other, and after a few seconds Benny leaned in.

"I'm not in trouble, am I?" he asked with a half-smile.

This struck the old man as funny, and he chuckled lightly. "No, Benito, you no in trouble."

"How are things going, you know … over da other place?" he continued, puffing away at his cigar.

Benny knew immediately what he was talking about. He was asking about his rail operation.

Benny nodded and smiled. "It's going great. We had a few issues, but I took care of it."

"You need any help, you ask me, OK?" Carmine said, patting Benny's hand.

"I will," Benny said.

"Benito, you a good boy. You remind me of your father in many way." Carmine sighed and continued patting Benny's hand. "You go back to work now. Good things … They come you way soon."

Benny smiled. He went back out to the front of the pizzeria and started making pies. He knew the little chat was more than it seemed. Carmine Mancini would never have such a short conversation without there being something more to it. He asked about the rail operation. He obviously knew it was going well just by the envelopes he was getting every week. Benny took less for himself and gave more to the boss. This was, of course, a calculated strategy. The more money in the envelope, the better Benny looked. Even if the boss found out, would it matter? All they understood was the bottom line. As long as Benny kept the money flowing, he was in good standing. Still, Benny sensed something that he couldn't put his finger on.

That was answered that night as Benny was on the phone taking an order. He hung up just as the underboss, Lou Santisi, walked in, surrounded by three tough-looking men that Benny didn't recognize.

"Benny," Lou said, reaching out his hand and shaking Benny's. "Let's walk."

The pair started slowly walking down the sidewalk. Benny glanced at the Soda Shoppe but did not see Taffy. Lou noticed the glance right away and smiled.

"Everything OK with da Centofanti girl?" he said, nudging Benny.

Benny grinned. "Sure, she's kinda great."

Lou sighed. "Ah, young love. I remember those days, so many years ago. Enjoy them, Benny."

The two walked down to the end of the block away from the gathering crowd around the pizzeria and soda shoppe.

"Benny, we got something that needs done," Lou said leaning close to Benny.

"OK, of course," Benny replied in an accommodating voice.

Lou paused, looked around, and lit a cigarette. "Benny, someone's gotta go."

Benny felt weak. 'Someone's gotta go meant that they were asking Benny to kill.

Lou leaned in close and whispered to Benny. Lou, like the rest of the organization, was constantly on edge about being recorded. Nothing was ever discussed openly in a normal voice. Anything of grave importance was never discussed where the FBI or local police could record it.

Lou practically whispered in his ear, "The priest. Frank Gallo.

Our Lady of the Rosary Church on the Eastside. Make it happen *You*, make it happen. No subcontractors, *you*."

Benny looked at Lou, surprised. "Father Gallo?" he whispered.

Lou nodded solemnly, leaned in again, and said, "Benito … I can only tell you so much. This man rapes children, children, Benito." His teeth were clenched tightly as he instantly raged. After a second, he took a deep breath, and his demeanor returned. "He uses drugs and has jeopardized this thing of ours in a way that cannot be forgiven. He is making noise when he should be silent. Benito, you make it happen."

Lou walked away leaving Benny standing on the corner in shock. He kept his poker face the best he could, but this was something that hit him like a clap of thunder on a beautiful day.

"Kill a priest? A priest? Fuck." Benny didn't know if he said it out loud or thought it in his head.

A car drove by blowing its horn and shook Benny out of his paralysis. In an instant the night seemed heavy, and the commotion and tightness of the street felt suffocating. The pizzeria was full of people as Benny walked back in and headed for the bathroom. Once inside he splashed water on his face and looked at himself in the mirror.

"Are you a soldier? Did you take an oath? Will you obey?"

He sighed, dried his face, and went back to work making pizzas. As soon as the rush ended, he picked up the phone and dialed the Soda Shoppe.

"Little Soda Shoppe, this is Moe."

"Hey, Moe, it's Benny. Taffy around?" he asked.

Moe giggled. "She sure is. Hang on, Benny, I'll go get her."

A minute later, Taffy picked up the phone. "Hi, Benaroo! What's shakin', bacon?"

This made him smile despite his now dismal mood. "Hey, Taf, can I come over later?"

"Since when do you need to ask, silly. See you after work," she said and hung up.

He felt like he had to speak with her. This was a very bad thing, and he was unable to see a way out. He knew deep down he had to tell Taffy. Of course, this violated omertà, and for this reason alone, he may be executed. He was going to have to take this risk.

CHAPTER 24
MORAL THOUGHTS

Thunder and lightning pounded the hills miles west of Youngstown as midnight approached. In short order the storm would be over the city cleansing the streets and dumping badly needed fresh water into the polluted river. Benny sat up on the window ledge looking out into the distance. The lightning was becoming more frequent, and the wind was picking up.

"What's wrong, baby?" Taffy asked from the kitchen. She was making them hot cocoa spiked with peppermint vodka.

"It's going to storm," he said.

"I know. There's a tornado watch, but don't worry, I have the candles ready in case the power goes out."

She came into the living room holding two oversized mugs and sat with him on the sill. The apartment was dimly lit and smelled of chocolate chip cookies. Taffy had them baking in the oven thinking they would be perfect with the cocoa.

She handed him one of the mugs. "Baby what's wrong? You seem a little off. Everything groovy?"

He smiled at her for using the word *groovy*. Of course she knew this would make him grin, which is why she used the no-longer-cool word to begin with.

"I talked to Carmine Mancini and Lou Santisi today," he said.

"Oh, yeah? Aren't those your bosses?" she asked, sipping her cocoa.

"Uh-huh." He shifted himself to face her. "Taf, they asked me to do something for them. Something I'm not sure I can do."

She looked at him puzzled. Of course she was well aware of what he did, and frankly she didn't really care. Is what he did any different than the corporate white-collar men who rob little old ladies of their life savings? As far as Taffy was concerned, those corporate bums were far worse. Benny ran gambling operations and loaned money. She knew he dabbled in stolen goods and had something to do with one of the unions at Sheet & Tube.

Of course, none of these things were any different than any other big city in America. Maybe everyone wouldn't see it the way she did, but she respected him for going out and getting what he wanted. She was proud to be seen with him and proud to be on his arm. He was Benny Squitteri, and he was all hers.

The silence dragged on until finally Taffy pushed him a little. "What is it, doll?"

He leaned in close to her. "They want me to kill someone," he said, quietly and firmly in her ear.

She pushed him away and stared at him, emotionless. The cocoa in her tummy seemed to turn icy cold, and she felt light-headed.

"They what?" she said, dismayed, as if she had misheard him.

"Yeah ... Taffy, they asked me to," he repeated, quietly.

"Who? Why? Benny ... What do you mean? What does that mean?"

He shrugged and sipped his cocoa. "It's part of this thing I'm in."

"I know that, Benny. But ... I didn't know you did *that* kinda thing!"

"Do you know Father Gallo over at Our Lady of the Rosary Church?" he asked, quietly.

"I know the church, but not him. I went to a wedding there once; I remember because the air conditioning was broken, and it was really hot in there," she said.

He took a deep breath and paused. "Taffy, they want me to take care of Father Gallo."

"The priest! Jesus fuckin' Christ, Benny, a priest?!" she nearly shrieked.

"Don't let the collar fool you, sweetheart. He's not what he appears, at all. He's ... he's a very bad man, Taffy."

"What?! How? What do you mean?" she asked, leaning into him.

"I can't get into specifics, so you'll have to trust me on this. OK? Trust me," he said.

"OK, Benny. I will. I trust you," she said.

"He rapes children. He does drugs and steals. I can't tell you how they know these things, but they are true. There's more that I can't get into with you, but there you go," he said, looking out the window at the approaching storm.

"What are you going to do?" she asked him.

"Taffy ... I can't do it ... I can't kill someone. I'm not a killer," he said with his head hanging low. "Even a man like this ... a man that is pure evil. I'm just not sure I have that in me."

She reached out and held his hand and squeezed. "I'm not going to pretend to understand, Benny, but what happens if you refuse? What will happen?"

"It's not a choice, Taffy. Carmine Mancini scares me more than God does."

At this, she began to cry. "Benny, this is bad shit," she sniffled out.

"I know, baby ... I know. I'm a thief and a gangster, Taffy, but killing a priest. Fuck."

She took a deep breath and choked out, "They'll kill you?"

He nodded his head. "Yes. I chose this life a long time ago. These things, the real bad things, were always for a few specific guys. Very dangerous men. I'm not sure why they asked me. Testing my loyalty, maybe?"

"Can we leave, Benny? Just leave?" she asked desperately.

He smirked and said, "And go where? New York City? Pittsburgh? Some fuckin' hillbilly town in Tennessee? How much cash do you have saved up? How long do you think before they track us down? This is a matter of principle with them. Hundreds of years of tradition on the line. Can you live looking over your shoulder every day of your life? If we have kids, then what? A new identity for them ... for us? Eventually they will find us."

She almost said, "What about the police?" but she bit her lip before it came out. Even she knew what his answer would be. He would never go to the police, and after a quick second, she realized she wouldn't either.

She reached over and hugged him just as the rain began to fall in sheets across the city. They embraced as she looked out the window at the silhouettes of the smokestacks that lined the river turning purple as the flashes of light danced in the sky.

They held onto each other for a minute when the tiny bell from the oven rang. Taffy got up and went to the kitchen, wiping her tears as she went. Silently she opened the oven and plated the cookies. Neither one spoke.

"How the fuck did it get to this?" Benny muttered, finally.

She sat back down and handed him a cookie. "I don't know, Benny. I do know that I love you, and that's not going to change."

They held each other as the storm raged across the city.

CHAPTER 25

THIS I DO FOR YOU, MY LOVE

She always slept with her window open. Even in the winter, when the Ohio weather was cold and brutal, she would at least crack it. Ever since she was a child, the sounds of the city lofting through the apartment soothed her like some strange lullaby—a lullaby she both loved and hated. The trains and the mill sounds were like a drug she had been taking since she was still in a crib. She wondered what would happen if suddenly the mill noises ceased, and she was left to lie in complete silence? Would she go crazy? The thought was not particularly comforting to her.

The rain had stopped an hour ago, and the apartment was damp and cool, mimicking her mood. Benny had gone home to try to get some sleep in his own bed, and that was OK with her. She knew he was struggling with his choices and decisions. She tossed in bed and fluffed her pillow. The clock on the nightstand read 3:17.

Benny had confessed many things to her earlier that night, and she was still processing everything he had said. They wanted him to kill a priest. A bad priest. A priest that stuck his cock into small children. Perhaps the justice they wanted to hand out was better than anything the authorities would be able to do. She knew what that organization was capable of, and like everyone else in the city, she had a strange respect for it. Despite the obvious clarity of what they did being immoral and illegal, they had a certain place in Youngstown society. In many ways, they were the sword of justice for times when the legitimate system failed its people. They were law and order when law and order was futile.

The patter and dripping of the rainwater carried on in the dark. Outside a car roared by in the night. She could hear the tires rolling and splashing through the puddles that had ponded in the street. Almost absent-mindedly, her hands found their way to her breasts, and she began to lightly squeeze and pull at her nipples.

His voice haunted her. "I'm not sure I can do it."

Her breathing was deep and steady as her mind began replaying what Benny had told her.

"I'm not a killer, Taffy."

Without realizing it, her hands slid down to her tummy, and she was making small circles with her fingers around her navel.

"I'm a thief and a gangster, Taffy, but killing a priest, good or bad. Fuck no."

She gulped a deep breath, spread her long legs slightly, and put her hand into her panties.

"If I don't do this, Taffy … they will kill me."

She slid into her fantasies as her fingers slid inside of her. First one finger, then two. She began making small circles in her vagina while her legs stiffened.

"Taffy … I don't know what to do …"

Her mind drifted, thinking about Benny and his mouth kissing her stomach, then her pussy.

"Carmine Mancini scares me more than God does."

Her thoughts slid back to Benny and how he came on her chest, and some got on her face the last time they fucked. She stiffened up and at the moment of her orgasm, she thought about the priest and killing him.

She lay still with her fingers warm and wet. A train horn blasted from down along Wilson Avenue, rolling and echoing its way through Brier Hill. She pulled her fingers out from her vagina and absentmindedly put them in her mouth without much thought.

The solution was not overly complicated and somehow was strangely alluring to her. In Taffy's mind, he wasn't really a priest but a child rapist that dressed up as a priest. A costume to hide what he really was … a scary monster that used God as a tool and pawn for his deviant pleasure. God may not punish this man, now … but Taffy knew she could.

And what if they did just leave the city? Then what? This Father Gallo man would still be here, still raping children as Benny had said. This was not an option for her.

Murder was wrong. She knew it, and so did everyone else. Would they kill Benny if he didn't do what he was ordered to do? Yes, they would. The Mancini organization was ruthless and unforgiving. The thought of Benny being gunned down on the street, or worse, made her stomach turn.

She took a deep dark breath and closed her eyes. Her mind was made up. She would do her due diligence in finding out everything she could about this Father Gallo man, then … she would do what she had to do to protect her man. She would be clever and cunning, careful and precise. She would be a hunter and a predator—her only prey, him. She loved Benny enough to protect him from the Mancinis. It occurred to her that Benny may not find out about what she planned to do. What if he didn't? Would that be a bad thing? Her secret would die with her, and the only person who would know would be a certain dead priest. The Mancinis would be placated, and the world of Taffy and Benny would continue on, uninterrupted.

Outside the rain began again in fits and starts. Her fingers made their way back down to the wet little circle on her underwear. Her secrets spun in her head as she closed her eyes. Her world was about to change.

CHAPTER 26

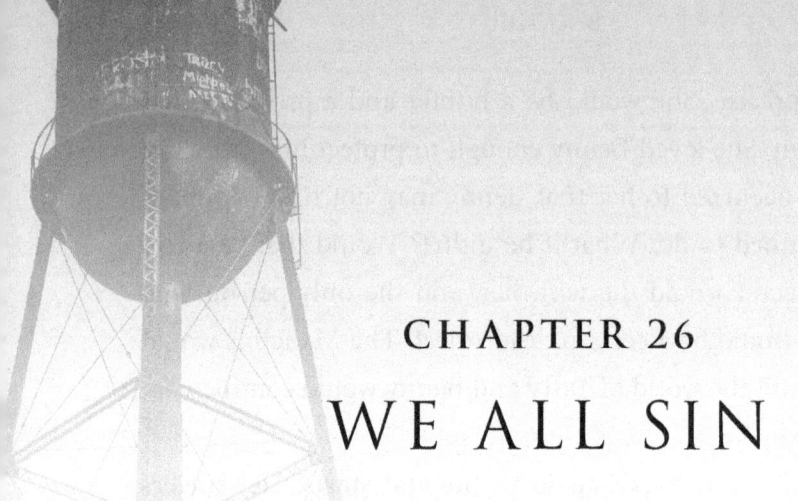

WE ALL SIN

Mass at Our Lady of the Rosary started at nine thirty sharp. Taffy blended in with the rest of the Catholics filling the sanctuary, ready to be forgiven for another week of sins. She sat toward the back, her eyes locked onto Father Gallo. She watched his every move and gesture with the secret knowledge that this holy man who the old people regarded as the next best thing to God was really a wolf in sheep's clothing.

When the time came for the mob of Catholics to receive the body of Christ, Taffy stood up and got into the line. As she made her way to the front, her heart began to beat faster and faster.

"The body of Christ. Amen."

She breathed deeply as she took one step at a time.

"The body of Christ. Amen."

Her hands locked at her tummy as she walked forward, step by step.

"The body of Christ. Amen."

She stood in front of him. Her mouth closed. Father Gallo looked at her and repeated the four words, "The body of Christ."

She stared, her mouth closed. Father Gallo stood there looking at her, the eucharist between his fingers.

"The body of Christ," he repeated, a little more firmly.

She narrowed her eyes and slowly opened her mouth. In blasphemy of all that is holy, she slowly pushed her tongue out and slowly licked her lips before he placed the wafer on her tongue.

"Amen," she said seductively, looking at him, her eyes narrowed in a lethal stare that immediately made him uncomfortable and nervous.

Father Gallo gently placed the body of Christ on her tongue. In a flash he had an urge to drop the chalice and run out of the church. He could run as fast as he could to Willy's house on Williamson Avenue. He would sprint across the Market Street Bridge, his arms and legs flailing. He was broke but not to worry, Ol' Willy would extend the holy man credit, right? With his little bag of white powder in tow, he could easily sprint back to the rectory and fix in the bathroom. Who would miss him? He could tell everyone that he felt ill and needed to step away from the service. They would all understand, wouldn't they? After all, even men of the cloth get ill.

That sweet relief of heroin coursing through his veins was all he needed to erase the thought of a strange girl that just made a mockery out of the sacrament. Soon enough Mass would end, and he could go see his personal savior. His name is Willy, not Jesus but Willy, and he would make everything OK.

After Mass ended, Taffy left feeling triumphant and emboldened. She could see how upset she made him, and that feeling was palpable. The next week, between her job and seeing Benny, she spent her free time following and watching the priest. In short order she knew everything she needed to know. His drug use was easily confirmed; she followed him to a house on Williamson Avenue several times, and it didn't take a genius to see what was happening. His lust for children had yet to be confirmed, but she did notice he stopped at Pemberton Park a lot and watched the kids playing on the swings. His priest's uniform provided perfect cover, and most of the adults paid little to no attention to him. He sat on the bench reading a newspaper and sipping a soda. From across the playground, close but not too close, Taffy watched his eyes scan the little girls almost continually. Other than that, his routine was set and semimundane. He shopped at Valu King once a week, he went to lunch twice a week with another priest, and he visited his garden twice a day—once in the morning and once after dinner. He got his gas at the Sohio Station on Phelps Street, and like everyone else, he played the Bug on Wednesdays, his ticket, bought at the newsstand across from city hall.

Benny had to work the following Saturday night, as did Taffy. She was scheduled at the Soda Shoppe until nine, and Benny was at LaVilla until eleven. He said he had some business after work but shouldn't be late. She nonchalantly shrugged and told him to come over after he was finished, no matter what time it was. He agreed, gave her a quick kiss on the cheek, and walked across the street to LaVilla.

As soon as she got off work that night, she took a quick shower and after a minute of thought, jumped in her car and headed across town to see what her buddy Father Frank was up to. As luck would have it, as soon as she pulled onto Wilson Avenue just a block from the church, she saw Frank pulling out and heading in the opposite way. She went another block, turned around, and went after him. At the next light she was two cars behind and kept following.

Across from Wick Park on the north side of town, a huge house in an affluent neighborhood, seemed to have too many cars in the driveway. She parked along the park close to the playground and sat in her car. Through her windshield, she watched Frank get out of his car and walk into the house. He was dressed in street clothes and a baseball cap. She nibbled on her fingernails, watching him.

The streetlight bathed her car in a gentle yellow glow. A few people walked by, mostly couples holding hands, talking, and laughing. She decided to see what she could see, so she gently pushed the car door open and stepped out. A fire truck turned down the street with its lights and siren on. Anyone that was around turned to look. Taffy took this as her chance to sprint across the street and blend into the darkness between houses. The darkness hid her well, and she stood frozen watching the firetruck go by; the few people along the park started walking again, oblivious to Taffy.

The big house that Frank disappeared into was two doors down from her. She walked quickly through the backyards and ended up on the side of the house. From the house behind her, a dog barked and ran along its lead.

The windows dripped soft light, and she froze as the back door opened, and she could hear two men out back talking. "Have you seen Chuckie around? I called him to see if he'd be here tonight, but he didn't answer."

She could smell cigarette smoke lofting around and surmised they were just outside to smoke. After a minute, she heard them go back inside.

Below one of the windows was a wheelbarrow that was full of

what looked like peat moss. Taffy quietly flipped it over, spilling its contents, and placed it below one of the windows. She gingerly climbed up on the wheelbarrow and balanced herself. Carefully peering into the window, she didn't see anything other than a few sex toys on a small bed. She narrowed her eyes and noticed a little stuffed dog in the corner and what looked like some type of restraining belts hanging on the closet door. A dog collar was hanging on the doorknob and a little pair of girl's pink cotton underwear.

"What in the fuck?" Taffy whispered to herself.

She was getting impatient and nervous standing there on the wheelbarrow, and her legs were starting to cramp. Then, she saw a fat man walk by the bedroom clad in dirty boxer shorts and a T-shirt. He was pulling a small girl by a thin chain attached to a leather collar around her tiny little neck. A quick second later she watched Father Gallo follow the pair holding what looked like a horsewhip. She stood on the wheelbarrow, slack-jawed and disbelieving.

How long did she stand there? Who knows? At some point she jumped down and made her way stealthily back to her car. She had seen all she needed to see. She was now judge and jury and very clearly in her head just sentenced Father Gallo to death for this and other obvious reasons.

She sat in her car and cried. "Cocksucking, fuck," she whimpered.

Tear- eyed and shaken, she stared at the house for a long moment. The car roared to life, and she sped down Wick Avenue toward Brier Hill. Just as she passed Youngstown University, she pulled into a parking lot in front of a payphone. She began dialing the Youngstown Police Department, then stopped. Gently, she laid the phone back on the handle.

What was the point, she surmised. They arrest him, the church circles its wagons and puffs its chest out in vanity, and the good Father Gallo is simply transferred to another church in Waterloo or Denver, or wherever the fuck they want to send him. He settles in nicely and before you know it, his cock is in another child. No, she would take care of Father Gallo herself.

One thing she was sure of; this was Father Gallos's last trip to that house.

CHAPTER 27
DECISIONS

Later that night, she ran into Benny in front of LaVilla just as they were closing up for the night. She hugged him and refused to let go. Her fingers dug into his back as she held onto him for what seemed like dear life.

"Baby, you OK?" he said, chuckling.

"I'm just so glad to see you," she said, staring at him intently.

He looked at her with soft sympathy. "Don't worry, baby. We'll figure everything out," he whispered to her reassuringly.

Quickly he changed the subject. "Do you want to sleep over? Or maybe I'll crash with you?"

She lied and told him that she wasn't feeling well and wanted to sleep alone at her house.

"Sure, baby, whatever you want," he said. "Maybe tomorrow night we can go get dinner if you're feeling better?"

"Benny, that would be fine. I'm sure I'll be better by morning. I think I just have a stress headache. I'll be fine by morning," she said, smiling at him.

The little white lie really wasn't too far from the truth. Her head ached, and she felt dizzy and sick from what she saw earlier that night.

Looking like a defeated fighter, she walked the stairs up to her apartment with her head hanging low. Once inside, she took three aspirins and put the teapot on the stove. She brewed some elderberry tea and sipped it in the solitude of her apartment.

She had tissues in her hand as she sat on the toilet. Her somber mood continued uninterrupted as the shower warmed up. She dabbed herself off before dropping her clothing on the floor and going into the warm water. Her sobbing was muffled by the sound of the water as the tears came effortlessly.

After showering, she went to her room and put on her pajamas. With a quick snap of the volume button, she turned the radio on to WHOT and settled into bed as the Moody Blues sang about knights in white satin. In her head, she saw the fat man holding that little chain. She saw the restraints on the door, and she saw that useless fuck Father Gallo. Tuesday she was going to pay a little visit to Father Gallo and straighten this bullshit out once and for all. Her best hope was to fix Father Gallo and get Benny off the hook with the Mancinis at the same time. She thought it possible if all the pieces fell into place just right.

That night she dreamt she was a little girl again, walking with her mom, a woman she had never met and had only known through old black and white photographs. In her dream she held her mother's hand as they walked through a field of vibrant, colorful flowers. Neither one spoke, but Taffy could feel her mother's love. She turned, and her mom was gone. The wind picked up, and the flowers started shedding their pedals. Taffy was surrounded by color and the fresh fragrance of the pedal. She closed her eyes, and the world seemed to explode in brilliant colors.

She awoke sometime before dawn and felt at peace. Her path was set, and she knew there would be no going back. Her legs swung slowly out of the bed, and in a quick motion, she was on her knees against the bed. She prayed to God:

> *Dear God, please protect me and guide me in this journey. God, give me the strength to bring justice to those who need it, and please, God, protect Benny and me from those who would do us harm. Amen.*

CHAPTER 28

PAINT YOUR GARDEN PINK

Our Lady of the Rosary Parish sat like a strange and ancient icon overlooking, judging, and condemning the city. The church itself sat on a small hill just east of downtown and had since 1913. The back of the church sat on a small rise that was buried deep in trees and barely visible from the neighborhood around it. There was an elegant garden with a large fountain and rows and rows of beautiful flowers. In the spring the scent of flowers was so thick that it might make you dizzy and weak in the knees. Honeysuckle lined the back patio while perfectly kept rose beds circled the fountain. The hedges that lined the garden were meticulously well kept and created a natural fence that blocked off the outside world, including the ugliness of the steel mills. The lawn was lush and perfectly manicured by the grounds staff that did the yardwork three times a week. In 1925, Father Antonio DelPrizzio began to hang wind chimes in the garden. Some fifty years later, that custom remained, and even when the slightest breeze carried itself through the garden, and the chimes would dance and giggle.

The priests of the church like privacy and solitude, and for years they had used the back courtyard for private meetings and as a sanctuary for meditation and prayer. Many of the policies, financial decisions, and political choices were made by the powerful Catholic diocese and local politicians in that garden.

What many of the people in Youngstown couldn't understand or didn't want to understand was that the Catholic Church was its own branch of organized crime. Instead of a bribe, it was a donation. A payoff was simply a gift for the poor. Kickbacks were pledges for the new recreation center being built down the street. In Youngstown, everybody got in on the act one way or another. The Mancini family used the fear of violence, the police used the fear of punishment, while the church used the fear of God. One hand washes the other, and the other.

Father Gallos's private residence in the rectory had a large double back door that went out into the garden. Every morning, before the church staff arrived, Frank would have his coffee with a small shot of strega. He would walk the garden, pondering his duties for the day and what needed to be done. As the week drew to an end, and Frank saw the weekend coming, he thought about two things, his sermon on Sunday and the young pussy he was going to fuck Saturday night. Only one of these things got his cock hard and gave him something to look forward to in his otherwise drab and trite existence.

On a Tuesday morning as Frank was walking the garden, Taffy parked her nondescript Ford sedan three blocks away in a parking lot used for the YMCA. Her car blended perfectly with the hundreds of others that filled the lot. Just before she got out of the car, she looked at herself in the rearview more and smiled. Her hair was pinned up underneath a Sheet & Tube baseball cap, and she wore no makeup. Dressed in plain jeans and a light gray sweatshirt, she could have been any girl in the city.

Early that morning she got up with Benny. He had to go to Cleveland to run some errands for his boss. He had mentioned staying in Cleveland for lunch and wouldn't be home until close to dinner. As soon as he left, she dressed and headed out the door.

The walk to the church took just a few minutes. Taffy kept her head down and didn't make eye contact with anyone she passed on the sidewalk on her way to the church. Stuffed down the front of her jeans was a long-barreled Smith & Wesson that was just one of the many guns her father owned. In a moment of Taffy-like oddness, she thought to herself how arousing it was that the barrel of this gun, this killing tool, was so close to her clit. She smiled and made a little mental note to fantasize about the feeling.

She looked around casually, turned, and walked up the small street behind the church. Nothing was on this backstreet other than two old warehouses; Taffy assumed they were both abandoned, and no one would be in them. They looked as if they might even be condemned. The street dead-ended into an old steel barricade, and the hill that the garden sat on was easily climbable for her. She took a casual look around, and not seeing anyone, she comically scurried up the hill to the side of the church.

Crouched like a cat burglar, she edged her way along the wall until she could see a small, unused gate at the corner. The gate was rusted and looked as if it hadn't been opened in years. She gave it a small push, and to her surprise, it opened easily with a small squeak.

"Well, damn," she whispered.

Just as she was slowly pushing her way through the gate, she heard his voice, and in that instant, she barely noticed the little spot of urine that she let go.

Frank was slowly walking toward her, holding his coffee cup and beaming. "Hi there! Are you lost? Nobody is here yet, but can I help you?"

She froze. "Ummm ... no, I don't think so. I was just ahhh ... Are you Father Gallo?"

"I sure am." He smiled, grandly.

Then, in an instant of panicky recognition, he remembered the girl from Sunday's service. She had licked her lips before she received communion. He froze; instinctively he knew something was wrong.

Little puffs of breath came from her, and the world seemed to move in slow motion. Her body turned numb. Her hands and feet seemed to turn to ice while the barrel of the gun seemed to be vibrating on her clit. They stood across from each other, both breathing heavily.

She could barely hear him from the ringing in her ears, and the sound of a train horn echoed in her head, loudly.

"You OK? You look pale," he said, with false concern and panic of his own.

Then, she stiffened as if someone electrocuted her. All the noise went away, while the world came into focus, and everything was somehow just. It was as if God looked down at her and nodded. Thy will be done, my child ... Thy will be done.

She pulled the gun from her crotch and aimed it directly at his face. He was just a few feet from her, guaranteeing a clean shot. She did not close her eyes, and she did not speak.

Father Gallos's eyes widened as he saw the gun. He instinctively knew he was a dead man.

In a harsh whisper he rambled out, "I am a child of God."

Taffy clenched her teeth and spit out, "You're a child of shit."

He made the sign of the cross and mumbled to himself, "Nel nome del padre, del figlio e dello spirito santo."

He then closed his eyes and prepared to answer to God.

The crack of the shot was instantly lost in the sounds of the mill just a few blocks away. No one noticed the sound, had anyone heard it, it would have been just another industrial cry from the Sheet & Tube plant.

His head exploded violently in a fine pink mist that in that instant filled the garden with new and beautiful color. Most of the back of his skull ended up in a neat, triangle pattern across the lawn while strange chunks of brain matter seemed to twist and spin in all directions. A large piece of his brain landed in the honeysuckle, hung on for a second, and fell to the ground with a gentle splat.

Father Frank fell in a heap of sin and debauchery on the lawn, his coffee cup still in his hand. Taffy gasped and looked around. She took a few steps toward him and looked down at the carnage like a child might look at a dead animal in the woods.

"Well, God damn," she muttered. "God have mercy on you. Fuckin' idiot."

A silent little voice in her head spoke, firmly, "Time to go, Taffy. Stay calm ... stay focused. Go Taffy ... Go!"

She backtracked her steps carefully and cautiously, and in short order she was back at her car. No one had seen her, or if they had, they didn't notice her. This, she was sure of. Sitting in her car, she focused on her breathing and tried to center herself.

"OK, Taffy, you know what's next," she mumbled.

What was next was getting rid of the gun. She had already found a place to do this; she just needed to get there calmly and slowly. No red flags, no red alerts. She pulled the gun from her pants and put it under the seat.

Fifteen minutes later she was underneath the Crescent Street Bridge. Even in a sea of steel mills, this part of the river was barren and isolated. The homeless would sometimes camp here, but the police generally drove them out. Much to her relief, as she turned the corner below the bridge, nobody was in sight. She parked the car and disassembled the gun into three pieces plus the five remaining bullets. Quickly, she jumped from the car and threw all the pieces into the river. She made sure to throw them in different directions and different distances, and the bullets she tossed in a handful as far out as she could.

She decided to take the long way home. She was scheduled to be at the Soda Shoppe at noon, for her long day. Her head was clear, and she seemed to be euphoric in an odd way. Thoughts bounced back and forth between her two hemispheres like some strange tennis match. Whatever she just did, she can't undo it.

She had yet to decide if she was going to tell Benny or not. She didn't want to keep any secrets from him, especially something this big, but she also needed to protect him. Benny would have to be told and told soon if that was going to be the case. That was going to be tricky; she knew his reaction might not be understanding.

Had she done it for him? For them? For herself? Maybe, but the lone idea that this priest raped children was enough of a reason. Could she have called the police again? Yes, but in this world, the church would have surrounded him, and at best he would have been removed from the parish and sent to another town to rape again. This was the only way, and in her mind, she was saving a child, she was saving Benny, and she was saving herself. As far as she was concerned, her soul was still clean. Her hands may be bloody by man's standards, but her *soul* was clean.

Grinning, her breathing came into its normal rhythm as she drove across Market Street Bridge toward the uptown. Her windows were down, and she smiled in triumph as she cranked Rod Stewart and sang along.

CHAPTER 29

THE WICKED ONE SHOWS ALL

"Father Gallo?"

Nothing.

"Father Gallo?"

Still nothing.

"Father!"

Sister Mary Margaret furrowed her brow as she called out for Father. Her voice echoed around the large sanctuary of the church. "ather … ather … ather."

Usually, Father Gallo turned on the lights and unlocked the doors for the staff every morning. Today, she had to use her key to get in, and the lights were dark.

The click of her shoes echoed as she made her way up to the altar, from there she could go down the currently dark hallway that would take her to the rectory and his private residence.

Mary Margret had been his assistant and confidant ever since Frank got assigned to the parish. She knew him well, and she knew this was unusual for him. Maybe he had fallen ill or just slept in, she considered. She had noticed that sometimes he did seem to sleep more than usual and often at strange times.

"Father Gallo?" she called out while knocking on his door.

With a tiny click, she turned the knob and went in.

"Father? Are you here?" she asked, cautiously.

She could smell the fresh garden as soon as she stepped in, and with some relief she thought, *Oh, good, he must be in the garden.*

Making her way through the rectory, she stopped dead in her tracks. On the kitchen counter were stacks of 4x6 photographs in several neat piles. One of the little piles was bound with a rubber band. Confused as to what she was seeing, she picked up a stack and froze. The top photograph showed a girl being choked with a bra and a group of men standing around. The girl had tear stains on her cheeks and small bruises on her budding breasts. She flipped to the next picture, and it showed a group of four or five men standing over a girl, all smiling with their arms around each other. She covered her mouth as she immediately recognized one of the men as Father Gallo.

"Dear God. No. No. No," she said, shaking her head slowly.

She stomached the picture and looked at one more. This one clearly showed Father Gallo smirking as he lay on top of the young girl.

Close to the pictures, sitting in the microwave, she caught sight of a needle and a bag of what looked like flour. Even this naive nun knew what the setup meant. She watched *60 Minutes* like everyone else and knew what she was seeing.

"Father?" she called out with a slight tone of anger in her voice.

She stepped outside into the sunlight. Covering her eyes, she took a second to get them adjusted. In a flash, she saw Father Gallo spread out on his back. She gasped and screamed but was unable to move.

"Dear God, no. Dear God, no," she prayed out loud.

He was almost unrecognizable. The back half of his head had cascaded across the garden, and a large hole was just below his right eye. The flies had already begun circling and landing on the large pool of blood in the grass.

Sister Margaret backed up slowly, turned, and ran into the rectory to call the police. Just as she grabbed the phone, she froze and spun to look at the pictures and the drugs. In that instant she knew that they were probably tied into him being killed. In a very quick instant, she did all the scenarios in her head and concluded that protecting the church and its reputation were paramount. If the pictures told just half the story, Frank Gallo was not what he appeared to be. God forgive her, but she knew what needed to be done.

She grabbed the pictures and the white powder and ran out the door, through the sanctuary, and to her car. She put all the paraphernalia in her glove box and ran back into the church. After doing a search of the rectory and not finding anything else incriminating, she called the Youngstown police to report the murder. While waiting for the police, she knelt down on the kitchen floor and prayed vigorously for Father Gallo. May God have mercy on his soul, and hers.

CHAPTER 30

ALL'S WELL THAT ENDS WELL

Taffy turned the corner onto Turin Street and saw the street packed with cars and people. The Soda Shoppe was busy, of course, and the pizzeria, the bank, and the store on the corner were too. She pulled her car around the back of the Soda Shoppe and parked in the little lot that she shared with the apartment building behind her. She ran up the back stairs, two at a time, that led up the rear of the building and into her apartment. As soon as she slammed the door, she began stripping off her clothes in fits and starts. Breathing deep, she leaned against the fridge clad only in her bra and underwear. Her jeans, socks, and shirt sat in a little pile at her feet.

"Fuck me," she exasperated.

Just then, the phone rang making her jump.

"Hello," she answered.

"Baby, where have you been?" It was Benny. "I've been calling all morning. Are you feeling better?"

"I'm sorry, doll, just out killing some time before my shift. Everything OK? Are you still in Cleveland?"

She heard him sigh on the other end of the line. "Yeah, yeah, just worried about you."

"Well, don't." She smacked. "Besides, I should be worrying about you."

Benny laughed, knowing she was right. "Pick you up at ten tonight?"

"OK, see you at ten. Remember not to park in the handicap space. Mrs. Underwood has her sister staying with her, and they need the spot."

Benny laughed. "I won't. I have to go to the pizza shop for a bit, anyway now that I'm thinking about it. Just walk over when you're done."

"Benny," she said while blinking tears out of her eyes, "Benny, mi piaci da morire."

Instantly Benny replied, "Taffy, anch'io ti amo da morire."

They hung up, and Taffy breathed a deep sigh and smiled. "Fuck," she said, happily.

While absently thinking about Benny, she loaded her clothes into the washing machine, and after a second of thought, took off her bra and underwear and threw them in too.

Standing naked in the bathroom, she quickly adjusted the shower as hot as she could take it. The shower was washing the trace amounts of blood off of her and seemed to be cleansing her mind at the same time. She washed every single inch of her body, twice. Under her nails and between her toes. She had read enough murder mystery books to know never to leave trace evidence. She scrubbed her face vigorously to the point that it hurt.

After showering, she dressed in her Soda Shoppe uniform,

adjusted her baseball cap with the ice cream cone on it, and closed her eyes.

In barely a whisper, she choked out definitely, "I'm a killer. I have killed."

She stared at herself in the mirror feeling strangely pacific and numb. Her head was screaming that what she had done was a sin, a crime, and unforgivable. But a calmer and more passive heart was telling her that this … man …, Frank Gallo, was a liar, a drug addict, a thief, and worst of all, a child abuser and rapist. That little band of words played in her head. Child. Rapist. Child. Rapist. Child. Rapist.

"Fuck him," she whispered in defiance to herself.

Ten minutes later, Taffy bounced into the Soda Shoppe smiling as usual. She began scooping ice cream with the other girls and chatting and gossiping away like any other day. With her hands full of ice cream cones and sodas, she went over to the tables closest to the windows and started handing out the orders. As the last sundae was put on the table, she looked up and froze. A Youngstown police car pulled up in front of LaVilla, and two officers got out, looked around, and went inside.

CHAPTER 31

I MISS YOU, DADDY

Taffy ducked out of work early, jumped into her car, and sped off to see her daddy. She didn't have to meet Benny until later that night, so she took the opportunity to see her dad and try to clear her head and stay focused.

The weeping willows lined the small roads that weaved their way through the cemetery. Their hanging branches guided visitors through the maze of roads and tombstones. She slowly drove through the catacombs to a familiar spot.

Her father's grave was set among the thousands of others at Lake Park Cemetery. Her visits to see him were becoming less frequent as the months and years ticked by—something that Taffy was aware of and somehow knew her father would understand.

Taffy-girl. You have you own life, now. You go and be happy and no worry about me. I with your mama, and we finally together again.

She parked and walked over the manicured grass to see her daddy.

"Hi, Pappa," she tearfully whispered while sitting down in front of the stone.

Hi Taffy-girl. How you doing, baby?

"I'm OK, Daddy, but I miss you so much," she choked out.

Aw, Taffy. I always around you. Even though you no see me, I'm there wit you. You know this, right?

"Yes, Daddy," she said firmly, between sobs.

She lifted her head to the sky as her tears pooled in her eyes. She blinked, and they delicately rolled down her cheeks.

"Oh, Daddy …" She cried. "I did a bad thing."

I know, Taffy. You gotta understand, Taffy. God, He judges, not me.

She cried. "I know, Daddy. But I did what I thought was right, and you once told me that if I did what I felt was right in my heart, then nobody could judge me harshly for it. Do you remember, Daddy? Do you remember when you told me that?"

I remember Taffy-girl.

"Daddy, I did what I thought was right. Do you think God will understand?" she said, sniffling.

I no sure, Taffy … I no sure. I am sure you heart remain pure. You do what you know was right. You tell God when you see him. You explain to Him, and He will understand.

"Oh, Daddy, I love you so much." She cried, hysterically.

I love you too, Taffy-girl. Now you go. There is so much of your life to live.

"OK, Daddy. I'll try to come see you more, I promise," she said, wiping away her tears.

She stopped at the chapel at the small sanctuary in front of the cemetery and lit a candle for her dad. She prayed for him and asked God to watch over him and her mother. She lit a second candle for Father Gallo and asked God to understand why she did what she did.

CHAPTER 32

SILENCE IS GOLDEN

That night, Taffy waited to meet Benny at LaVilla like they had planned. The pizzeria was crowded, and people were bouncing back and forth from the LaVilla to the Soda Shoppe. Taffy watched her girls from the sidewalk taking care of customers and laughing while making sodas. A little pat on the back was delivered from her to herself. She chatted away with people while waiting for Benny, gawking at the cars full of people driving up and down the street.

Benny pulled up, and Taffy jumped in. They headed out of Brier Hill and landed at the Hub Restaurant, downtown.

"Anything you want to talk about?" she asked, stirring her tea.

"Not really, and hey, I don't want you to worry, Taffy. I'll do my best to figure something out about my little problem," he said, sadly.

"Bullshit, Benny. This is *our* problem; *we'll* figure something out."

She was torn between telling him about what she had done and letting things run their course. She kept her mouth shut, knowing it was best just to let the chips fall and deal with things when they did. She hated the look on his face. A look of sadness and worry. She wanted to scream out, "I killed that fuck! Don't worry about your boss or that fuckin' cock-sucking priest because I ventilated the back of his head!"

She sighed, sipping her tea and watching Benny stare out the cafe window. Soon enough, he would hear about the priest being killed, and then what? She wasn't sure what would happen then. Would he be angry? Sad? Confused? The answer to that question would be answered eventually, but for now, she remained silent.

CHAPTER 33
OMERTÀ

The murder of Father Frank Gallo rocked the city to its core. The headline from the *Youngstown Vindicator* screamed in bold print. "PRIEST MURDERED. VALLEY IN SHOCK." The Catholic Diocese released a statement condemning the killing as a "cowardly act of evil," and urged the guilty party to turn himself in. That evening the top story on all three local news networks was the murder. Youngstown Police Chief Carl Morris gave a statement vowing to hunt down the killer at any cost. He asked anyone with any information to please come forward. When a local reporter asked about a motive, the chief replied with "no comment at this time."

Wednesday morning Taffy was downtown on Hazel Street buying a few new houseplants for her apartment when she heard the cry of the newsboy.

"Extra! Extra! Local priest murdered at Our Lady of the Rosary!" the kid called out as people gathered to get a paper.

"Oh, fuck me," she whispered.

Taffy flipped the kid a dime and took a paper. She hurriedly jogged back to her car, jumped in, and slammed the door. Her eyes darted back and forth reading the story. When she had read every word, she read it again.

"Fuck me," she said, dryly.

Not a word about her, Benny, or even a motive. Taffy, the clever girl she was, knew it was only a matter of time before the priest's extracurricular activities would come to light. Soon enough a sneaky reporter from the *Vindicator* would discover the priest had a drug habit, and worse, a fetish for young girls. Obviously, this would point the police in an entirely different direction than her or Benny.

Ten minutes later she cruised through her Brier Hill neighborhood and onto Turin Street. She didn't see Benny's car at the pizzeria and surmised he must be out working. She pulled around the back of the Soda Shoppe, and there she saw his car.

"Oh," she muttered and parked.

As soon as she parked, Benny stepped out of his car. He was holding a rolled-up newspaper. She got out of her car and stood toe to toe with him.

"Was this you?" he asked stony faced. His voice was just above a harsh whisper.

"Benny ... I. I ... Benny," she stammered.

"Taffy, was this you?" he demanded.

She stood there with her mouth hanging open, unsure of just what to say.

"Fuck, Taffy. That's where you were yesterday morning, wasn't it? Don't fuckin' lie to me, Taffy. I mean it."

She kept choking on the air, not sure what to say.

He grabbed her by the arm and pulled her across the small gravel parking lot to the back door of her apartment.

"Ow! Benny that hurts," she cried, trying to keep her balance.

"I'm sorry, Taffy," he said, letting go. "I'm sorry. C'mon, baby."

They went into her apartment, neither one saying a word. He locked the door as soon as they were inside.

"Do you want coffee? Soda?" she asked, walking into the kitchen.

"No, Taffy," he said firmly from the living room.

He looked out the window to the pizza shop across the street. Nothing was really happening there, other than the Riverbend delivery truck parked in the side alley delivering staple goods.

"Sit down," she said, pointing at the couch.

"I don't want to sit down, Taffy," he said, still irritated.

She stood in the doorway holding the newspaper in one hand and a cherry soda in the other.

She sighed deeply and held her breath for a second. "Benny, I did it."

Benny lunged at her and covered her mouth. She dropped both the soda and the paper. "Don't say it," he whispered in her ear.

He pulled her into the bathroom and shut the door. He picked her up and put her on the vanity. He grabbed her face and put his mouth next to her ear. "You don't know who's listening. Don't ever speak out loud like that again, Taffy."

She nodded obediently. They were nose to nose. Benny grabbed her by the scruff of her neck and turned her head to the side and spoke in a whisper into her ear. "You did this? You killed that fuck?"

Taffy turned and looked into his eyes. She nodded her head quickly. She had no fear or remorse on her face.

"Taffy … Taffy … why, baby?" he whispered.

She shrugged and looked away. The silence spun out until she whispered in his ear. "Benny, I can't lose you. You said it yourself—if you don't kill him, they'll kill you. I couldn't let that happen. Benny, I did this for us … I did it for the countless children he ruined, and I did it for God."

"Taffy, if they find out you killed him, and not me …" he whispered in an exasperated voice.

She grabbed his face with both her hands and kissed his mouth. "How would they find out? Who would tell them? Benny, he's into some bad shit, you know that. Anyone could have done it."

"Anyone *could* have, but you *did*," he whispered, brutally. "And if they find out I disobeyed an order, and I told you about it … Taffy, they'll kill us both."

"Omertà?" She whispered in a natural, thick Italian accent.

"Don't fuck around, Taffy. Not with them, believe me," he said quietly.

She reached out and squeezed him, her mouth gently resting on his ear. "It's done now. I couldn't unring that bell even if I wanted to. You understand that, don't you?"

He smiled. "Lo faccio, e ti amo. Questo è il nostro tempo e il nostro mondo."

Taffy bit her lip and smiled back at him. "Anch'io ti amo. È il nostro tempo e il nostro mondo. Siamo io e te, Benito."

That night the rain came in a steady patter against the windows in Benny's loft. He rolled over and could make out her body in the soft light from the windows. Occasionally a flash of lightning would expose her in a strange blue aura. She moaned and rolled over, twitching as she did. His head spun and spun as the thoughts spilled out. *Is she brave, or is she weak? You're sleeping next to a killer. You know that, don't you?*

Jimmy Taaffe

The sheets hugged her shapely body. Her hips rounded from her stomach to her thighs. He was in love with everything about her. Her smile was his treasure, her laugh was of the gods, her eyes … those eyes … Her breasts were full and her large areolas, perfect. And that magical place between her legs that was so perfect for him.

CHAPTER 34

SHOULD HAVE BEEN MORE CAREFUL, LITTLE GIRL

Inside the old warehouse, across from the back of the Our Lady of the Rosary Church, Jimmy Bacala stacked boxes of stolen goods against the wall. There were more boxes now than ever before. He didn't ask questions, but he concluded that the Mancinis had found a new source of stolen goods. The temperature was rising already, and it was going to be a scorcher. The back sliding door was open, allowing a little early-morning breeze to blow in, but the front remained closed to keep up the illusion that the building and the one next to it were vacant.

These two buildings were used by the Mancinis to temporarily store stolen goods and other items. The warehouse was huge, and at first glance, it looked like any other neglected building on the east side of downtown. A small driveway around back snaked its way to an old railroad construction road that was abandoned. This was the only way for trucks and cars to get in. Anyone just passing by would assume the buildings were vacant. The buildings being on a dead-end street only helped to secure the isolation and ruse that was needed. In reality, the inside was well kept and full of miscellaneous items. In the back corner two cars sat parked nose to nose—one Lincoln Continental and a Cadillac Brougham. These cars were just a small part of an auto theft ring that operated primarily on the south side of the city. Stacked up neatly were hubcaps, car radios, and two rows of brand-new radial tires.

Jimmy's only job was keeping track of the items that came into the building and going out. He had a small notebook in which he wrote everything down. Of course everything was written in his own strange code and could only be translated by Jimmy himself. Boxes of watches, household goods, and clothing were meticulously stacked in neat piles. Jimmy ushered the fences in and ran the warehouse like a well-oiled machine.

He grabbed a push broom and began to sweep the warehouse. He thought about asking Dominic Capetti if he could hire a kid to help around the place, sweeping, running errands, and so forth. He doubted Capetti would let him, but he planned to ask just the same.

Jimmy stretched his back and winced. He was a fullback at Wilson High School just a few short years ago, and on one fateful Friday night against Chaney, he went down and hurt his back. His football career was over, and years later, the pain lingered on and on. He walked and stretched like he always did.

The front of the building had a small row of dusty windows; vines and other foliage covered the aged brick. Jimmy looked out and just caught sight of a tall girl sporting a baseball cap, walking down the sidewalk. She was looking right and left, then finally focusing on the little hill that went up to the church. Jimmy pulled out a cigarette and kept watching her with mild curiosity. Nobody came down the dead-end street unless they were lost and needed to turn around. The girl took one last look right and left and then scampered up the hill. He took a deep drag on his smoke and continued to stare up at the church, slightly confused on what this girl was up to. She disappeared behind the row of hedges that lined the back of the church.

"That's weird," he mumbled to himself.

He stood there blowing perfect smoke rings while thinking about washing his car later that day. His wife had also mentioned dinner at the Living Room Restaurant with her sister and her husband that night. On top of everything, their cat, Smuckers, needed to go to the vet.

Just then he heard a shot come from the church, startling him out of his stupor. Most people wouldn't recognize the sound from the mixture of steel mill sounds that floated through the city, but Jimmy did.

"Holy shit," he said wide-eyed.

He watched the girl walk quickly down the hill, stuffing a gun in her crotch. She walked quickly but didn't run. Her steps were deliberate and coy as if they were rehearsed. As she passed in front of the building, she took her hat off and wiped her forehead.

"Holy fuck," Jimmy gasped.

He saw her face and knew exactly who the girl was. Her name was Taffy, and she owned that little soda place across from LaVilla over in Brier Hill. She was the girl that ran with Benny Squitteri. They had gone to school together or something. Last week he took his kids there for ice cream, and she waited on them. His wife commented on how pretty she was and how impressive the soda shop was. He gave her a nice tip, and she gave his kids balloons.

"Jesus fuckin' Christ," Jimmy said, dumbfounded.

He stared out the window and watched her walk down the street and out of sight.

He shook his head and started sweeping the floor again. An hour later he heard the wail of sirens getting close. With a deep sigh he walked around to the front of the warehouse and stood on the sidewalk with his broom. He knew the cops would be snooping around the area, and he didn't want them knocking on the warehouse door. If he stood out front, they could just talk to him without the need to go inside. Sure enough, twenty minutes later an obvious detective walked around back looking at the ground and around the church. He spotted Jimmy and walked across the street.

"What's going on up there?" Jimmy motioned to the church.

"Trouble. Looks like it might be a killing," the detective said, taking a drag from his Marlboro.

He looked at Jimmy and pointed to the church. "You see anything strange or unusual this morning?" he asked, with an air of gentle curiosity.

Jimmy shrugged. "No. Been here all morning; nothing unusual."

CHAPTER 35

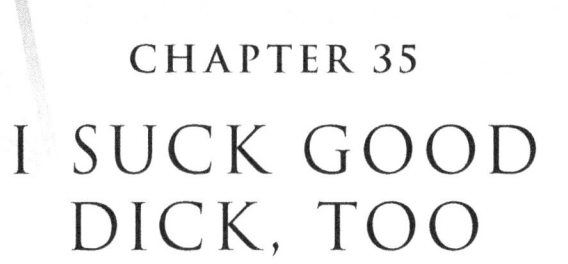

I SUCK GOOD DICK, TOO

Benny and Taffy were lying in bed, watching the eleven o'clock news. The funeral of Father Frank Gallo was, of course, the top story. They lay there watching the funeral procession on television as it made its way from Our Lady of the Rosary Church to Oak Hill Cemetery. The reporter questioned many people, who all appeared to be in tears and gushing out condolences.

"Do you believe this shit?" Taffy remarked with a look of disgust on her face.

Benny smiled. "Fucked up. What do you think these people would think if they knew the truth about the good Father Gallo?"

"Shit, I doubt they would care," she said.

"Taf." Benny leaned into her. "What was it like, you know, killing?"

She looked at him for a long second. "You want some complicated and meaningful answer?"

"No. I just want to know how you feel about it," Benny said, shrugging.

"I don't feel anything, really. I can sleep fine at night knowing this man will no longer be hurting children. My heart is, and my soul is intact. Father Gallo can fuck off."

She looked at him with a wisp of a smile on her face. "You cool with that answer?"

"Sure," he said.

Taffy crawled to the end of the bed and flipped the channel to another local station. Same thing, the funeral of Father Gallo.

"Damn, this guy is famous as fuck," she said.

"Don't worry, baby. Watch how quick people forget about this," he said.

Benny changed the subject. "So, how's everything at the Soda Shoppe. Girls all OK?"

"I guess so. Been busy, which is good," Taffy said, fluffing her pillow.

"Oh, guess what?" she said, excitedly.

"Do tell," Benny said.

"Ralph asked Moe out, you know, on a date," she said, with raised eyebrows.

"Yeah, I know," Benny said, smiling.

"Wait, how do you know? What did Ralph say?" She giggled, hitting Benny with the pillow.

"Nothing," he said, shielding himself from the pillow. "Just that he's excited. He already asked about us doubling with them. Maybe we can scoot down to the Jungle Inn for dinner?"

"Really? Benny, that would be so much fun!" she said excitedly.

"He likes her, I guess. He says she's cool and a lot of fun, blah blah blah," he said, already losing interest in the conversion.

"She brags about her dick-sucking skills, so Ralph has that to look forward to," she said, slyly.

"No way they are as good as yours," Benny said, with a slick grin.

She smiled reaching over to the nightstand, grabbed a hair tie, and put her long black hair into a ponytail.

"I give better head than her," Taffy said, pouting.

Benny smiled and nodded. "I have no doubt, you do."

"You ready?" she said, reaching over to turn off the little lamp on the nightstand.

In an instant, Father Gallo and the rest of the world were lost as the two fell into each other.

CHAPTER 36

THE RAT

"Jimmy Bacala is here to see you, Carmine," Lou said.

"Who?" Carmine asked, looking somewhat perplexed.

"Jimmy Bacala. He runs the warehouses over on the east side, across from the church. He's OK. He does a good job for us. Says he needs to talk to you."

Carmine wiped his mouth with a napkin and nodded his head. "OK, send him in."

Carmine stood up and straightened himself. He cleared his throat and stood at attention like a general.

The door opened, and Jimmy nervously peaked in. "Mr. Mancini. I'd like a minute if I could."

Carmine smiled and waved him in. "Jimmy. Come on in. How things going at the warehouse? I hear you doing a good job over there."

Jimmy nodded while shaking Carmine's hand. "Everything is good. Busy, that's for sure."

"Sit down, Jimmy. Can I get you anything? A soda pop? Coffee? A shot of anisette?"

Nervously, Jimmy waved his hand dismissively. "I'm OK,

Carmine." He looked at the plate of unfinished food and cringed. "I apologize for interrupting your lunch, Carmine."

"Nonsense, Jimmy. Sit down, sit down." Carmine leaned forward. "What's on you mind, Jimmy."

Jimmy drew a deep breath and anxiously began his somewhat rehearsed speech. "The priest, the one that was shot over …"

Carmine held up one boney finger and waved it back and forth. Immediately, Jimmy stopped talking.

He took that boney finger and put it on his lips. Jimmy got the picture.

Carmine and Jimmy walked out the back door of LaVilla and into the gravel parking lot.

Carmine leaned in close to Jimmy. "The FBI, they everywhere these days. No place is safe."

Jimmy nodded. "I understand, Carmine. Forgive me, I should have realized."

Carmine lightly grabbed Jimmy's arm. "Tell me, Jimmy. What do you know about the priest?"

Jimmy spent the next ten minutes telling Carmine about what was going on in the warehouse, how he was organizing the pallets of items that were coming in, and how he wanted to hire some help. Carmine hid his impatience well, giving Jimmy some wiggle room with his preamble.

"Forgive me, Jimmy. But what does this have to do with the priest?" Carmine asked, gently interrupting.

"I was sweeping the floor, and I heard a shot come from the church," Jimmy said.

"Did you tell da police dis?" Carmine asked, looking Jimmy in the eye.

In a semipanic, Jimmy spit out, "Of course not, Carmine. No! Never!"

Carmine smiled. "Good. Now go on, Jimmy."

"I looked out the window, and I saw the Centofanti girl, the one who owns the soda shoppe across the street and runs around with Benny Squitteri. I saw her walking away from the back garden where the priest was shot. I saw her stick a gun down the front of her pants."

Carmine stood motionless. "You sure it was da Centofanti girl?"

"Sure, I'm sure, 100 percent. You don't miss a looker like her," Jimmy replied quickly.

Carmine put his arm around Jimmy's shoulder and began walking him back inside the pizza shop.

"You keep dis to yourself. You understand me, Jimmy."

Jimmy shook his head quickly. "Of course I will, Carmine. I just want you should know. I'm not sure what's going on, but I do know she killed that priest, and she is dating Benny Squitteri."

Lou Santisi escorted Jimmy out of the pizza shop and watched him drive away. He then walked back to the kitchen.

"Where's Mr. Mancini?" he asked the young kid who was just punching in on the timeclock.

"He's out back," the pimply-faced kid said, pointing to the back door.

Lou went out back, and the two titans of organized crime sat on the loading dock with their feet, clad in expensive dress shoes, dangling off the dock.

"It appears Taffy Centofanti is doing a little more than selling ice cream sodas," Carmine said, looking down at his feet.

Lou looked puzzled. "What do you mean, Carmine? Taffy is a sweetheart. Benny brings her around a lot. I remember her father; he was a stand-up guy."

"Our friend Bacala tells me she did a little work for Benito," Carmine said, leaning into Lou.

"What are you talking about, Carmine?" a puzzled Lou asked.

"It seems as if Benny told his girl about our friend Father Gallo. It also appears she took it upon herself to fix our problem."

"Carmine, I find it hard to believe Benny would violate omertà," Lou said, quietly.

Carmine thought for a second. "Tuesday, where was Benito?"

Lou shrugged. "I sent him and Ralph Testa to Cleveland to pick up some money."

"They were gone all day?" Carmine asked.

Lou sighed. He knew where Carmine was going with this. "Yeah, they left early and got back late. Fuck."

Carmine closed his eyes. "Young love. She knows, Lou. She knows because Benito told her."

Lou spoke quickly. "What if you're wrong? What then?"

"I'm not wrong, and you know this, old friend. Tell me, underboss, tell me what you think happened," Carmine said, slyly.

Lou didn't speak for more than five minutes. Then, with a deep sigh, he turned to Carmine. "Perhaps Benny couldn't do it. You once told me all men can kill, but not all men are killers. Maybe he told her what we asked him to do and confessed he was unable to do it. Then what? She did for us what he would not or could not. If this is the case, I doubt he left anything out."

Lou looked sad as he continued to speak. "If he told her this, then what else has he confessed to his lover? He has many secrets, Carmine. Secrets that would destroy us all."

Both men sat in silence, absorbing what the situation meant. Both Taffy and Benny were guilty of breaking the laws set by years of tradition and culture. The penalty for such actions is death. Little did Benny and Taffy realize that at this very moment, their futures were being decided in a parking lot behind a pizzeria. The decision on whether they would live or die was being discussed at the same time Taffy was laughing while making ice cream sodas, and Benny was meticulously washing his GTO.

"What are you going to do?" Lou said, pressing Carmine.

"I don't know, Lou. I like Benito, but Lou, he has broken the sacred rule of omertà. This cannot be forgiven."

Lou sighed. "Carmine, let your decision be a sound one, not made in haste. Take some time to look at the options, eh?"

"Perhaps you're right, old friend," Carmine said.

"Jimmy?" Lou asked with raised eyebrows.

"He knows things he should not know. I don't like that he has this in his pocket," Carmine said, getting to his feet.

Two days later, Jimmy Bacala was found dead along the banks of the Mahoning River, not far from Our Lady of the Rosary Church. His throat had been slashed and his tongue removed.

CHAPTER 37

A BAD DAY FOR THE MAYOR

Sam Blystone was just about to leave his office at city hall when there was a quick knock on his door.

"Come!" he yelled while putting on his sports coat.

His secretary cracked the door and stuck her head in.

"Come?" she said in a sexy voice. "I'll come for you." She giggled.

Sam smiled. "What's up?"

She handed him a secure sealed envelope. "This just came via courier."

"Thanks, baby. Anything else?" he asked.

"Nope. OK if I scoot? I'm going to grab the kids, and Dale wanted me to cook corn on the cob for dinner," she said.

"No, no. Go ahead. Did anyone from the *Vindicator* call today?" he asked.

"Not that I know of," she said, closing the door.

Sam sat down at his desk and turned the envelope over in his hand. There were no markings, just a thick white envelope with a security seal on it.

He carefully broke the seal and pulled out a single index card. Written in plain handwriting, Sam read:

Mr. Mayor

In regards to our last conversation, the status quo will remain. The unfortunate portrait will remain a valued piece of our collection.
D.C.

Sam's stomach turned, and he felt nauseous. "Fuck. Fuck," he scowled from under his breath.

How could they ignore what he told them about Father Gallo? Was there to be no reward, no consideration? His first instinct was to drive over to that fuckin' pizzeria in Brier Hill and shoot that worthless fuck Dom Capetti. Had they not realized if he didn't come forward and tell them about Father Frank, that church would be bugged, and they would be finished?

"Lousycocksuckingdoublecrossingcocksuckingfaggots," he mumbled out in a quick succession of words.

He sat at his desk feeling deflated, angry, and depressed. The slow realization of what this meant was beginning to take hold. That fuckin' picture ... he chastised himself again for his own weakness and lack of self-control with that man and many others, not to mention his secretary that he had been fucking.

"God dammit," he whispered.

Father Gallo was dead, and Sam knew God-damn well who was responsible. These people killed a priest at the drop of a hat. What would they do to him if he made waves? His family? His wife, Joyce? He had to play the game at any cost and any reward.

As usual, he took the long way home. With every passing minute the reality of his situation was becoming more and more stifling. For the first time in a great many years he felt like crying. He knew when the Mancinis first showed him the picture it was bad ... very bad, but Sam knew eventually he would figure a way out. Telling them about Father Gallo was the way out he needed. Now that that card had been played, he was stuck. He punched the steering wheel when it dawned on him that he also got them the shitty motherfucking Fosterville bridge project.

"Cocksuckers!" he screamed out in frustration and desperation.

Sam pulled onto his cul de sac, and his neighbor Marty was out walking his dog. He looked away from Sam in a strange way.

Sam nonchalantly gave a polite wave that wasn't returned and pulled into his driveway. The garage door was closed, which was unusual. Usually Joyce kept it open as she ran around the house and the yard doing little tasks and watching the kids.

He jumped out of his car and opened the big garage door. His face twisted with confusion and puzzlement looking at stacks of his clothes and personal items thrown in the garage.

"Joyce!" he bawled.

Her face was twisted in a weird combination of rage and sadness. She stood in the door that led from the kitchen into the garage. She had a bundle of his suits in her arms.

"Joyce! What the fuck?" he yelled.

"Fuck you!" she screamed in an articulately cold voice.

She threw the clothes into the growing pile on the garage floor and ran back into the house. Sam waded across the piles of his stuff and into the kitchen where she was standing with her arms crossed tightly across her chest. Her tear-stained face was red and puffy.

"Where are the kids?" Sam asked, feeling even more confused. "What the fuck is wrong?"

"You cocksucking faggot," she hissed.

Sam stood there dumbfounded. "What are you talking about? What's wrong?" he pleaded.

She reached across the table and grabbed a stack of 8x10 photos. The first one she held up showed him and his secretary kissing in his car. She held it up for a few seconds making sure to get her point across. She slammed it down on the table with a smack and held up another. That picture showed them hugging with her hand on his crotch.

"Did she get your dick hard?" she hissed. "Does she let you cum on her face?"

"How did you get those?" he asked, starting to feel faint.

"Fuck you," she said holding up another picture.

This one showed the pair outside of a restaurant kissing each other. She slammed it on the table again.

Sam stood there dismayed and defeated. He was at a loss for words. Somehow, she had figured out that something was going on with him and his secretary. *Who could have told her?* he thought lightly.

She stared at him with fire in her eyes. Her hands shook ever so slightly while she blindly reached for the next picture.

These pictures were the crème de la crème.

She held a picture up, shaking slightly with her breath coming out in choppy little puffs.

"Oh my God, Joyce. I'm … I'm … Let me explain," Sam said, on the verge of passing out.

The picture showed Sam and a good-looking young man kissing against the hood of Sam's car. The distinguished mayor's hand was down the front of the man's pants. Joyce stared at him, repulsed.

With painfully slow and deliberate movement, Joyce reached for one more photograph. The picture was taken through a cracked window between the curtains. Although the picture was dark and slightly grainy, it clearly showed Sam naked, a man behind fucking him.

Joyce took a deep breath and spoke smugly. "I wonder how the city will feel about their squeaky-clean mayor now? And by the way, I took the liberty of letting all the neighbors know, even gave them copies of the pictures. After all, they should be aware that their neighbor is an adulterer and a faggot."

Sam stood stony-faced and numb. Something broke in him in an almost audible snap. He shook his head and pushed past Joyce and down the basement stairs. Behind the workbench was a small wooden box with a little lock on it. He grabbed the box and twisted the lock off with a screwdriver. Inside was a .22 revolver.

He walked calmly up the stairs and into the kitchen with the gun hanging in his hand.

"I want you out by the end of the day, faggot," she whispered and started to continue her tirade. "If you think the kids are ever going to see their—"

That was it, Sam raised the gun, and before she could even blink, a popping noise filled the kitchen, and a small red hole appeared in the middle of her chest. She gasped in almost comical surprise and fell backward.

"Cunt," Sam mumbled, walking out the door into the garage.

He began rummaging through his belongings on the garage floor, tossing clothes to the side. He grabbed a pair of jeans and a T-shirt, stripped out of his suit, and dressed in casual clothes. With the garage door open, a few of his neighbors were out front on the sidewalk watching him. They leaned into each other whispering about what was going on at the Blystone house. He walked back into the kitchen and looked down at Joyce. Her eyes were open, glassy and lifeless. He thought of the time when they first started dating. They decided to drive to Chicago for a little vacation. The car broke down outside of Akron, and they had to hitchhike home. Oh, how they had laughed.

"I'm sorry, baby," he whispered.

He tasted the gun oil in his mouth just as he pulled the trigger, and his world went dark and cold.

As it turned out, the Mancini family wasn't the only one interested in Sam's extracurricular life. Joyce, on the good advice of her suspicious father, had hired a private investigator to look at her husband. It took less than two weeks for Joyce to get hit with the hard reality of her husband's true personality.

The death of Mayor Blystone and the subsequent details of his personal life rocked the city of Youngstown and made national news. It even knocked the murder of Father Gallo off the front page. Rumors swirled around the city about extramarital affairs and Mafia assassinations. The bars along Poland and Wilson Avenues all buzzed with chatter from the steelworkers about possible conspiracy theories and a connection between the assassination of Father Gallo and the death of the mayor.

Brier Hill

At Patsy's Bar on Wilson Avenue, Lonnie Mcalister barked over the jukebox to anyone who would listen. "Goddamn mayor was probably stealing money from the church! That's how this thing ties up! You think it's a coincidence they both are dead so close together?"

Across the Center Street Bridge at Tooties Grill, two steelworkers were shooting a quiet game of pool. "Tell you what I think ..." Roy Fillmore said taking his shot. "That priest, Gallo, he was probably fucking the mayor's wife. This thing's gotta be connected somehow."

At Cute Clipz Hair Salon over in Brownlee Woods, Amanda Yonkers was getting her roots done.

"I'll tell you what, I've seen that Joyce Blystone. She looks like one of the hookers on Midlothian."

Vickie Walker kept dabbing the color onto her graying hair. Her gum snapped over and over. "That's what I've heard, a real tramp. Carol Kowalski is in her bridge club and says that she takes it in the ass, and ..." Vickie looked around to make sure nobody could hear her juicy little nugget of gossip, "I heard she told Carol that she lets him put his cum on her face."

Amanda gasped. "That hardly surprises me!"

The circles of gossip turned and turned around Youngstown.

Taffy sat in the back booth at the Soda Shoppe with the newspaper in hand. Benny walked in and sat down.

"Did you see this?" she asked.

"See what?" Benny asked as he reached over and grabbed her cherry soda and took a sip.

"The mayor killed his wife and himself!" she said, exasperated.

"Can I see that?" He pointed to the paper.

She handed him the paper, and they sat in silence as Benny read the article and shook his head.

"Wow. How about that," he said.

"Did you know him? … the mayor?" Taffy asked, sliding her soda back and taking a small sip.

"No, not really. I had met him once or twice just long enough to shake his hand."

"Our big, bad city," Taffy smirked.

"Hey," Benny said, changing the subject, "wanna go see a movie tonight?"

"Fuck yeah, I do," she said, smiling.

That night they drove over to the West Side Drive Inn and sat through *Close Encounters of the Third Kind*. Like a couple of teenagers, they sat close to each other in Benny's GTO, Taffy occasionally kissing his cheek. After the movie they sat at Knox Coffee Shop and sipped hot cocoa.

They couldn't seem to get enough of each other. Everything in the world was perfect now, and Taffy began to daydream of a future with Benny who was feeling the same way.

CHAPTER 38
NOT SO GOOD NEWS

Benny sat at the intersection of South Avenue and East Dewey Street, his GTO rumbling as he waited for the signal to turn green. He watched the black sedan two cars behind him in his rearview mirror. The car had been following him since he left LaVilla earlier. When the light turned green, Benny took off for Homestead Park. He saw the vehicle following him in his rearview mirror. The black sedan turned into the park as soon as he did. Benny pulled to the side and stopped. He inconspicuously felt for the pistol that was under his seat and in one quick move slid the pistol into his waistband.

Benny looked over and saw two men in suits in the car.

"You fuckin' want something? Who are you?" Benny demanded.

The driver of the sedan pointed across the park to a nondescript man dressed in overalls and holding a steelworker's helmet and lunch pail. Immediately, Benny assumed he was one of the thousands of men that worked in the mills. The man was buying a hot dog at the concession stand by the playground. He could have been the father of any of the hundreds of children playing in the park.

Benny shrugged. "What the fuck?"

The man in the passenger seat took off his sunglasses. "Benny, don't make me show you my badge. You never know who might be watching."

This answered one of Benny's questions. He sat stony-faced looking at the two men.

"Do yourself a favor, Benny. Go park your car and have a talk with him. I promise you'll be glad you did."

Benny didn't reply. He whipped his GTO into a parking spot and got out. He watched the sedan pull away and head back toward South Avenue.

Benny slowly walked to the man who was eating his hot dog. He scanned the park for anything unusual. Nothing seemed to jump out at him, just another beautiful day in Youngstown. The man saw Benny walking toward him, and he nodded. Benny nonchalantly adjusted the pistol he had tucked in his waistband.

"Benny Squitteri," the man stated, smiling.

"Do I know you?" Benny asked.

"Benny, I'm special agent Sam Cobb. FBI, Pittsburgh," the man said as they started walking slowly around the park.

"You can go fuck yourself, Agent Cobb," Benny said calmly. "I have nothing to say to you, and did the taxpayers pay for that disguise?"

"Oh, I know Benny." Cobb took a bite of his hot dog. "But I have something to say to you. And I would have gladly worn my G-man suit for everyone to see."

Benny stopped. "Funny. Spit it out, Cobb. I have a lot to do today."

Cobb nodded approvingly. "I like a man that gets to the point."

Benny smirked. "As do I, so get to the point."

"Jimmy Bacala is dead, but I'm sure you know this."

Benny said nothing.

"We figure your boss is responsible. Well, let me rephrase that, we know your boss is responsible."

Benny said nothing.

"I want you to hear something, Benny," Cobb said, turning toward his unmarked sedan.

They began walking to the car when Benny asked, "How'd you know I was coming to the park today?"

"You're a predictable man, Mr. Squitteri, and in your world that's a bad thing. We know you come here three times a week to walk. Good exercise, right?" Cobb said with a knowing smile on his chiseled face.

Benny smiled too, knowing this agent Cobb knew that although it was true Benny liked to walk here, occasionally he picked up Bug payments here, too.

They got to the car, and Cobb slid into the driver's seat. Benny stayed outside the car but leaned in the passenger window.

"Get in, Benny," Cobb said.

"Fuck off. I'll stay here."

Cobb shrugged and turned a portable tape player toward Benny and hit play.

Benny's heart began to beat a little faster when he heard the voices of Carmine Mancini and Lou Santisi. The sound quality was mediocre and sounded monotone, but it was easily understandable. Benny listened closely.

There was a little clutter, and then the voice of Lou Santisi. "Carmine, any thoughts on Romeo and Juliet?"

Cobb hit pause and smiled. "Funny they refer to you and Taffy

Centofanti as Romeo and Juliet. That's our code name for the two of you at the bureau, as well."

Benny wasn't smiling. He reached in and hit play, anxious to hear what was coming next.

"Romeo, he disappoint me in so many ways." Long pause. "I no see any way out of dis for him; he tells his girlfriend family business, murder we do. Who knows who she tells and where the gossip trail will end."

Lou Santisi's voice, "I'm afraid I have to agree with you, Carmine. You said it best, if he talks to one, he talks to all."

Benny grew even more angry when he heard the insult.

"I know you love Benny, but dis, dis we cannot forgive," Carmine said.

Lou's voice again, "You want me to take care of it?"

Carmine's voice was loud and clear. 'Si."

Benny was shocked. Carmine had been his mentor, a father figure, and his hero. What he heard next made him sick and dizzy.

Lou's voice once more, "What about Juliet?"

Without skipping a beat, Carmine's voice came out of the speakers. "She can go, too. I no trust her; her father, I no trusted him, either. The last thing we need is a heartbroken girl spilling secrets out of grief and anger. She goes, too."

Just then, in the background on the tape, church bells began ringing.

Despite the news he just heard, he smiled grimly and looked at Cobb. "You bugged the fuckin' church, didn't you?"

Cobb smiled and shrugged, looking triumphant. "My idea. We were actually one step ahead of Father Gallo."

Again, Benny reached in and hit the play button. Carmine's

voice rang out. "You take your time planning dis one. I want no fuckups, Lou. Take your time and get it done right. Try to get dem both at da same time."

Cobb stopped the tape and looked at Benny with a touch of sympathy. "Benny, they are going to kill you; obviously you know this. You just heard the tape. Perhaps you'd like to enlighten me on *why* they want you and Taffy dead?"

Benny leaned against the agent's car and lit a cigarette. Cobb got out of the car and walked around to Benny.

"How the fuck should I know?" Benny said, angrily.

"Benny, we can offer you and Taffy complete protection. Your time is up here; you must know this. You heard the tapes. You and Taffy are dead if you stay, and we know you can't run. We are the only option you have at this point, Benny. Think about it."

"I didn't hear shit. I heard you say you bugged the church, and that's it. You and the rest of you cocksuckers can fuck off," Benny said angrily and walked away.

"Benny, think about it!" Cobb called out. "Just think about it! Benny, we can't watch you 24/7!"

CHAPTER 39

BIG TROUBLE IN BRIER HILL

Benny pulled up to the payphone on Midlothian Boulevard and called Taffy's apartment.

He got no answer, so he called the Soda Shoppe, where Moe answered. "Little Soda Shoppe, this is Moe."

"Moe it's, Benny. Taffy there?" he asked.

"Hang on, Benny. I think she took the garbage out," Moe said, then put down the phone.

An agonizing minute later, Taffy answered. "Hi, Benaroo. How's my boy?"

"Taffy, listen, meet me at my mom's in Canfield," Benny said urgently.

"Wait. What? Now? Benny, why?" she said.

"Baby, just meet me there. Don't talk to anyone; just get in your car and go."

Just like that, in a flash of terror, Benny yelled into the phone. "Taffy, wait! No! don't start your car!"

Benny knew the Mancinis liked to use the Youngstown tune-up.

This was when dynamite was used to blow up a car with the person in it.

"Benny, Jesus Christ, what the fuck is going on?" she nearly screamed.

"Baby, go out the back door, cut through the buildings behind your place, and wait for me in the lobby of the doughnut shop. Stay in the lobby; I'll be there in ten minutes, and don't talk to anyone. Just wait for me," Benny instructed, sounding mechanical.

"OK, baby. I will. Do I need anything?" she asked, almost hysterically.

"No, baby. I'll see you in ten minutes," he said, and hung up.

"Fuck me," she whispered under her breath and hung up.

She ran lightly into the bathroom and locked the door. She splashed water on her face and looked into the mirror.

Certain realities were beginning to take hold. Obviously, this had something to do with her killing Father Gallo. Why else would Benny be acting like this? Did the police find out and question him? No, she didn't think so. She froze. She thought she peed her pants but wasn't sure. She stuck her hand down the front of her pants, and to mild relief, she hadn't. "Oh, fuckin' mother fucker, the Mancinis."

She burst out of the bathroom and ran through the little kitchen that led to the back door. She grabbed Moe by the shoulders. "I need you to watch the store. Can you do that for me?" she asked.

"Sure, Taffy, of course. What's wrong?" she said, her voice rising.

"I'll explain later; just do this for me, OK. Can you, Moe?" Taffy nearly screamed.

"Yes. Yes, Taffy!" Moe said, wide-eyed.

Taffy started for the back door and stopped. She turned around and hugged Moe tightly. "I love you, Moe," she said and bolted out the door.

Benny sped down Market Street toward Brier Hill. Traffic was heavy, but Benny was an excellent driver and navigated the semigridlock easily. He buzzed through downtown and up Belmont to Brier Hill. He got to the doughnut shop at the same time as Taffy. He saw her sprinting across the street and beeped the horn. She jumped in the car, and they sped off out of Brier Hill.

As Taffy was diving into Benny's GTO, the three FBI agents sat at Islay's Coffee Shop in the back booth.

"Well, thoughts?" The agent in charge of the Youngstown district asked agent Cobb.

Sam stirred his coffee. "Hard to say. I think now that he's heard the tapes, he'll figure out he and Juliet are out of options. It may take him a few days, but sooner or later, he'll get it."

All three men nodded silently. The lead agent looked at Cobb. "Can we tie Squitteri to the murder of Frank Gallo?"

"No. Not yet anyway. He might have a solid alibi. He and Ralph Testa were in Cleveland all day as far as we can tell. That doesn't mean he didn't orchestrate it, somehow. Plus, these people are so tight-lipped about everything. They never actually say anything that can incriminate themselves, and they speak in their codes and hand gestures."

The second agent, Riley Mohr, cleared his throat. "Is it possible, I don't know, gentleman, is it possible that the Centofanti girl was involved?"

None of the men spoke. Finally, agent Cobb spoke up. "I'm not sure about that. I'm not sure that would have been an option for the Mancinis."

"I'm not talking about the Mancinis; I'm talking about Benny and Taffy conspiring to kill Gallo," agent Mohr said, almost reluctantly.

"What's the benefit to that? I mean, why?" Cobb asked, rubbing his chin.

Mohr sighed. "I don't know, but my gut tells me there's more going on here than meets the eye. I think the Centofanti girl is somehow linked to this. I'm not saying she killed Gallo, but I think somehow, she's involved."

The three agents sat in silence pondering the possibility that Taffy might be involved in the murder.

"OK, riddle me this, gentlemen. Why does Carmine Mancini want them dead? Squitteri is a good earner, and he has always been loyal. Now, Carmine not only wants him dead, but his sweetheart, too," Cobb stated.

"Well, that's the million-dollar question. When can we get a bug into Centofanti's Soda Shoppe?" Mohr asked.

"We're working on the warrant now," Cobb said.

The waitress refiled their coffee as the conversion drifted away from Benny and Taffy and onto other issues involving the city of Youngstown.

Taffy and Benny drove out to Millcreek Park and headed up to Fellows Riverside Gardens. The massive garden was secluded enough that the pair could walk and talk about the day's developments without anyone hearing. On the quick ride to the park, they both remained mostly silent, lost in their thoughts.

Benny parked the car, and they got out.

"Do you want a pop?" he asked, looking at the refreshment stand across the parking lot.

She nodded yes; he took her hand and squeezed it. At this little sign of tenderness, she practically fell into his arms.

"Benny, what's wrong?" she cried out.

"C'mon. Let's walk," he said, forgetting about the pop.

They held hands and walked through the gardens, blending in with the other people enjoying the park. Benny was on edge, looking around for anything that might be suspicious. So far, all he could see was families and children admiring the rows of flowers.

"Listen, Taffy, they know. I don't know how, but they know," Benny said, sitting Taffy down on the edge of the big fountain.

Immediately, Taffy now understood what was going on. "The Mancinis? Carmine knows? Is it the police?" she said, desperately.

"Yeah, kinda both, maybe. The Mancinis for sure. I went to the park today, and this FBI agent cornered me and made me listen to a tape he had of Carmine and Lou talking about us."

Taffy gasped. "Us? Me and you? What did they say? Benny, what's going on!"

"I won't lie to you, Taffy; it's not good." Benny lit a cigarette and pushed on. "I listened to the tape and, uh," Benny looked around, "Carmine gave instructions to have you and me killed."

Taffy blinked in shock. "Killed?" She kept blinking, almost involuntarily.

Benny nodded and dragged his cigarette. "Yeah, baby, killed."

"My God, Benny. What does that mean?" she cried.

"It means exactly that. Somehow, they must have figured out what happened; I'm not sure how, but they did. No one saw you, right?" Benny stared at her for a long second.

"No! I'm sure, Benny. Nobody saw me," she said, exasperated.

"Doesn't matter," Benny said. "The wheels are in motion now."

"When? I mean fuck, Benny! How does this work? When do we have to start watching? When can we leave? Jesus Christ!" Taffy asked in near hysterics.

"Not today." Benny took another drag of his cigarette. "On the tapes Carmine said to plan it out and make sure everything was perfect. I'll know when something is off; I'll pick up on it."

"Well, now what? What the fuck do we do?" Taffy said.

"I don't know, baby. We have a couple options. None of them are very fuckin' good," Benny said, looking over his shoulder.

"Go," Taffy said, desperately. "Go. What are they?"

"We can, geez, fuckin' never thought I'd say this, but we can go to the FBI. They'll protect us. Witness protection and all that shit."

"The FBI?" Taffy nearly screamed. "Fuck, Benny. They'll own us if we do that. You know it, and so do I. What else, Benny?"

"Remember you asked me about leaving Youngstown? Just getting out? Well, we can leave, just go," he said, looking down at his feet.

Taffy stared at him, slack-jawed. "Can we? Can we, Benny?" She practically fell onto him, "Do you have any money? I do, not a million dollars, but I have some money, Benny, we can just leave this fuckin' city forever."

"Where do we go?" Benny asked, looking at Taffy.

"I don't know, Ben, someplace far from here. I don't give a shit if its fuckin' Timbuktu," Taffy said, shaking her head.

"What about the Soda Shoppe? The building? You own them both, don't you?" Benny asked.

"I don't care, Benny. I'll give them to Moe. Her and her folks can run the shop and have the building. They have been good to me over the years, Benny. Moe's mom always made sure I had food, and when my dad died, Mr. De Santo told me that he considers me to be a daughter. They are amazing people, and Moe will be great," Taffy said with tears welling up in her big blue eyes.

Benny nodded approvingly.

"How will they get us?" Taffy asked quietly, as the pair got up and continued walking slowly through the massive garden.

"You won't know." Benny sighed. "It'll be a comunione."

In her Italian accent, Taffy questioned, "Comunione?"

"Si, Comunione. That means they won't find us. Conferma means the bodies will be found. Capisci quello che sto dicendo, Taffy?"

Taffy nodded. "I understand."

"This is my fault. If you die, it's on me whether I'm alive or I'm dead. This is all my fault. I should have just killed that fuckin' priest and been done with it," Benny said.

"No, it's my fault. I killed that fuck Gallo. Maybe I just have let the police handle it? Maybe then we wouldn't be in this mess." She sighed, "It doesn't matter, Benny." She looked at him and kissed his mouth softly. "Io sono per sempre con te e tu sei per sempre con me."

That night Benny and Taffy sat in Benny's loft drinking beers with the television low. The Pittsburgh Pirates were playing the Cubs; the Pirates were winning. Benny had lowered all the lights and locked the doors using the industrial locks that were still working in the old warehouse. He had pulled the curtains so none could see in. On the coffee table between them was Benny's Browning 9mm pistol. Unbeknownst to Benny, tucked in her waistband, Taffy had a pistol, too.

"You said you have some cash," Benny said.

Taffy nodded. "Yeah. I do. Some of my dad's money and some I've just saved up."

Benny nodded. "I have a lot, Taffy. More than enough to start a new life, far away from Brier Hill."

Taffy chuckled. "That's a good thing; if we were broke, we'd be fucked hard."

They sat in silence watching the ballgame and drinking beer. They both were far away in their own thoughts.

Somewhere in her thoughts, Taffy felt the tiny coal of anger begin to glow. The little angry one decided to stomp on fear and take to the top of the hill prize. In her head, she began to look closely at the pieces that were falling into place like some weird jigsaw puzzle. Carmine Mancini, with the nod of his head, was able to kill her and Benny. Kill them. And for what? Disobeying his orders. Breaking the retarded law of omertà? It was 1977, not one hundred years ago in Italy. This was Youngstown, Ohio, and it was 1977. Fuck him and his cock-sucking fraternity of puppets.

Taffy stood up and clicked off the television with a snap. Benny looked at her, confused. "I was watching that, and I thought you were, too."

"How many other people is Carmine *going* to kill? How many people *has* he killed? Hundreds? Maybe more?" Taffy said coldly. "He's the one that needs to die."

Benny did not like where this was going. He watched her eyes carefully and didn't like what he saw.

"They want to kill us?" Taffy said with growing anger. "Those fucks."

"Taffy, you have no idea who you're fucking with," Benny said, in desperation.

Taffy bit her lip and narrowed her gaze, scaring Benny slightly. "No, Benito, they don't know who they're fucking with."

That night behind the locked doors of Benny's loft, Taffy climbed on top of Benny and lowered herself onto him. She slowly moved her hips in sweeping circles while listening to the sounds of the mills. The train whistles bounced around Brier Hill while the shift whistle blew into the night. She arched her back and screamed as her orgasm shook her body.

She grabbed his face with both hands with a mixture of despair and longing. "Foresti meglio a iniziare ad Amari da morire proprio oar, Benny. Adesso e per sempre."

Just as sleep knocked on her door, Deja vu washed over Taffy in an eerie, spooky, mirrored image of her dealing with Father Gallo. She rolled over and looked at Benny.

"Even if we leave, Carmine will find us, won't he?" she whispered in the darkness of his loft.

"Yeah. Yeah, he probably will. He has friends, Taffy. Lots of friends," he said, sleepily. "We'll have to be careful forever."

Taffy rolled over and stared at the ceiling. Her head spun in circles, and with a small smile she thought to herself, *Once a killer, always a killer.*

CHAPTER 40

A CHANGE OF HEART

The next day Benny went to work as usual; Taffy did as well. Throughout the morning, Taffy would stand at the window and wave at Benny with a sad smile on her face. Benny kept the front door locked and the lights on in the lobby. He pulled on the back door to make sure it was secure. They were now balancing a fine line between knowing what their fate might soon be and looking for a way to change their destiny.

Benny went into the back room and put on an apron. He pulled a hundred-pound bag of flour across the floor and opened it. Very carefully he began the process of making the dough for the day. His mind began drifting as he put the ingredients into the big mixer and started the machine.

He needed to be very careful the next few days, protecting himself and Taffy. He had seen enough of the calculated viciousness of the Mancinis over the years to know that he was, without a doubt, in grave danger. He had to play his cards just right. Taffy had enthusiastically agreed to leave the city behind and find a new life far away from Youngstown and Brier Hill. That was fine with him.

He added the yeast, water, salt, and sugar to the giant bowl mixture and turned it on.

Carmine Mancini is ready to toss him aside like garbage on the side of the road. He had put so many thousands of dollars into Carmine's pockets over the years, and Carmine was ready to kill him and probably never think of him again.

After a few minutes of the watery soup mixing, Benny began scooping flour into the bowl and watched the dough begin to take form.

He loved Taffy; he was sure of this. Carmine was ready to kill her, *Kill* her. He imagined her being shot and lying on the ground bleeding. She would be afraid, and she would cry. He tried to shake the nightmare thought, only it wasn't a dream. Carmine had already started the wheels turning. This was reality—a reality that Taffy was a dead woman, and he was a dead man.

After the dough had mixed and raised, he began cutting the dough and putting it on the scale, getting the weight just right. In his hands he slowly and carefully rolled the dough into balls and placed them on the metal tray. His mind raced.

He was a soldier, a loyal soldier that men counted on and depended on, sometimes with their very lives. His love for Taffy and his loyalty to his family were tangled in a melee of emotions. His angels and his demons at war. In his head he kept hearing Carmine's voice ordering his and Taffy's death.

"Cocksucker," he mumbled under his breath.

He told Taffy he couldn't kill anyone, and God help him that was true, but this anger was starting to slowly go from simmer to boil. She's a young woman with her entire life ahead of her, and this man with just a few words can have her killed.

They wouldn't find her body. That meant she would be stuffed into a barrel and tossed into the Mahoning River, or dropped into a shallow grave, like a sack of garbage. They would cut her body up into small pieces. Her hands and head would be removed. She would be naked on the back table of Castones Salvage Yard, where two unpleasant men would see her naked body, joking as they sawed off her extremities. There would be no funeral or calling hours. No one to mourn her.

Benny threw the dough cutter across the room. "Fuck!" he screamed in desperation and rage. "Fuck! Fuck! Fuck!"

CHAPTER 41

SAME PAGE

After their shifts had ended, they drove mostly in silence to a small restaurant for a bite to eat and to try to get their heads together.

"Can you go to Ralph? What about Mickey?" Taffy asked, while slowly stirring her blackberry tea.

They sat secluded in the back of Gino's coffee shop in Canfield. The cafe was far enough away from Brier Hill that nobody knew them. Gino's was a nice family restaurant with terrific pie and cakes. Benny picked at his raspberry pie and shook his head.

"No, their loyalty is with the Mancinis, not me. I don't blame them for that," he said.

In the back of Taffy's mind, she was glad to hear that answer. She had already begun a plan to take care of Carmine Mancini. Her anger and dismay for the way they ran their world sickened her—the fact that Carmine can, with a simple nod of his head, take the life of someone, most notably at the moment, them.

Little did Taffy know that Benny was on the same strange page as her. He too, despite his reservations with Father Gallo, had decided that she was worth killing for. She was a killer, and he was about to become one.

"Benny, is there any way out for us? I mean, is there anything we can do that even if it's crazy, might work?"

Benny shrugged and chuckled.

"What, Benny. Say it," she poked him in a weird kind of seductively sexy language.

"I'm going to kill Carmine Mancini."

She stared at him with just a hint of a smile on her delicate face. The corner of her upper lip raised slightly as she whispered, "Not if I kill him first."

CHAPTER 42

LET THE GAMES BEGIN

Benny picked up the phone at LaVilla and dialed Charlie Whippos's number. Charlie was Carmine's driver and not an especially bright man.

"Hello," Charlie answered, sounding out of breath.

"Charlie! Hey, it's Benny Squitteri," he said, pleasantly.

"Benny. How are you, pal. How's Taffy?" he said, still catching his breath.

"Everyone's good. You good? Andrea and the kids?" Benny asked.

"Yeah, yeah. All good. Andrea broke her foot, tripped on the front stoop," he replied, chuckling.

Benny grunted and said, "That's too bad, hope she's OK. Hey, you're still golfing, right?"

"Sure am. My games not very good, but I'm still swinging," Charlie said.

Benny sniffed. "Listen, I got a set of MacGregors for you, for that thing you did last winter, you remember?"

Benny was referring to some money that was owed to him by an acquaintance of Charlie's. Charlie stepped in and took care of collecting the money.

"Shit, Benny, that was no big deal. Glad I could help," he said.

"I know, Charlie, but still, take the clubs; I got a bunch."

"Well, sure, Benny. Appreciate it," Charlie said.

"Where you gonna be tomorrow? I can drop them off to you; I'll be running around all day, so I'll find you," Benny said carefully, so as not to arouse any suspicion.

A slight break in the conversion flow made Benny stiffen. Charlie was not the sharpest knife in the drawer, but he could still smell a rat.

"Ummm, let's see, I've got to run to a few meetings with Carmine; how about you meet me at Our Lady of the Rosary at say, nine thirty? Carmine has some business there, and I'll just be sitting in the car." Charlie laughed.

Benny smiled. "Perfect. See you tomorrow."

Early that night, Benny drove out to the Mancini construction offices on Albert Street. He knew no one would be there after five, and even if someone was there, Benny showing up wouldn't be out of the ordinary. The gate was shut and locked, but Benny knew if you drove around the side of the front office building, you could have access to the big pole barns in the back. Inside the barns were heavy equipment, traffic barrels, and other assorted construction supplies. He parked next to one of the barns, got out, and pulled on the door, which was, of course, locked. The front of the barn had huge sliding doors, which were needed for storage of the larger equipment. Without much hope, Benny gave the massive door a slight tug, and much to his surprise, it slid open just a few feet. That was all he needed.

The barn was dark, but the slice of fading sunlight was just enough for him to navigate around the big, open space. He made his way to the back office and into a storage room. He flipped the light switch and looked around the windowless room; in the corner was a special cabinet in which the humidity was carefully controlled. Benny opened the door and found what he was looking for. Carefully he pulled out a box with an explosive emblem painted on it. He laid it on the desk and opened a few of the tall cabinets looking through the contents until he found what he needed. He packed everything, turned off the light, and walked quickly out of the barn. His trunk was more than big enough for all the supplies. With precious cargo packed, he left.

As Benny was pulling out of the front gate and turning back onto Albert Street, he caught the flashing lights in his rearview mirror.

"Jesus fuck," he muttered and started to pull over.

The police officer walked up slowly to the car and leaned on the window "Hi there; you just pulling out of the construction company?"

"Yeah, I work there. Forgot my wallet in the office, but nobody is there; guess I'll have to wait until tomorrow to grab it."

The officer casually looked in the back seat and nodded. "What's your name?"

Cool as a cucumber, Benny looked directly at the officer and said, "Benny Squitteri. I've been with Mancini construction for a very long time."

That was all the officer needed to hear. He tapped the ragtop of Benny's car, "OK, Mr. Squitteri. Have a nice night and drive carefully."

Benny breathed a little sigh of relief. His next stop was back home to build his new little friend.

In the back of the garage was a workbench that was covered in greasy tools and car parts. Benny did his own tune-ups and oil changes, and despite the haphazard look of the bench, he knew where every nut and bolt was. He had the dynamite laid out and a book in front of him on explosives. The door opened with a creak, and Taffy peeked in.

"You in here?" she called out.

"Yeah, I'm here," he said.

Taffy walked around the car and stepped over a few boxes and a big floor jack. She stood next to him looking down at little pieces of wire, a few switches, and six sticks of dynamite.

"I thought dynamite was red," she said, curiously.

"I think that's just on TV and in cartoons. Clearly this fun stuff is tan."

"Can I touch it?" she asked quietly.

Benny carefully picked up one of the sticks and placed it in her hand.

"It's heavier than I thought," she said, holding it with two hands, then one.

"I guess so," he said, flipping the pages of the book that was in front of him.

"How do you know about all this stuff? You know, dynamite and explosives and stuff?" she asked.

"I really don't know all that much, to be honest. I used to work with a demolition crew at Mancini Construction sometimes. I picked up a lot there. You know, kinda the basics of demolition 101."

"Will it work?" she asked, looking down at the bomb.

"Uh-huh, no doubt, I'm that good," he said, smiling.

Taffy kissed his cheek, "I'll go make you something to eat real quick. Uhh, this is really happening tomorrow, isn't it?"

He looked at her in the dim light of the single, dirty lightbulb. "Yeah, yeah, unless you have second thoughts."

"No," she said, firmly. "Fuck, no."

"Can you make me a plate of ravioli?" he said, smiling.

"Si, Benito." She went up the stairs, and he snipped the final wire.

CHAPTER 43

I LOVE THE FUCK OUT OF YOU

The side window to the church was unlocked, and Benny, with just a little nudge, popped it open. He waited, holding his breath to see if an alarm would sound. Much to his relief, the church remained silent. Gently, he pushed the duffel bag through the window and climbed in. The church was lit only by a few votive candles from the front of the church and a few glowing exit signs. Once Benny's eyes adjusted to the dim light, he easily made his way to the back pew where Carmine sat and did business. Carefully and quietly Benny pulled out the perfectly wrapped bundle of dynamite and held it in his hands.

"Fuck," he muttered under his breath.

He gently put the bundle of destruction on the pew and pulled out a receiver and a small bracket he had fashioned from pieces of an old radio he found in Taffy's basement. He crawled under the pew and attached the dynamite and receiver using the brackets and some loose wire. He turned on the receiver and a tiny red light began to glow.

Ten minutes later, Benny roared through downtown on his way back to Belmont Avenue where Taffy was waiting. He made a quick stop at Augustinellis Bakery. He jogged around back and knocked on the back door. The owner was a friend of his, and Benny was able to grab a few pastries for later.

Back at Benny's loft, Taffy kept peeking out the window looking for her headlights to sweep across the side parking lot.

"C'mon baby, where are you?" she whispered to herself.

As if she summoned him, she watched his car pull in. She heard the garage door open and a car door close. A second later the engine was silent, and she again heard the garage door, but this time being closed and locked.

Benny trotted up the stairs holding a small box of pastries. Taffy opened the door and pulled him in. She shut the door and squeezed him.

"Baby I was so worried. Everything OK? Are you OK?" she begged.

"It's all good," he said, kicking off his shoes. "I brought you some pastries."

She laughed and kissed his cheek. "I love the fuck out of you, Benny Squitteri."

"I love the fuck out of you, Taffy Centofanti," he said, smiling.

They sat on Benny's couch nibbling the pastries and drinking milk.

"Did everything go OK?" she asked, almost reluctantly.

Benny nodded. "Yeah, actually easier than I thought. Even if he doesn't sit on the, you know, surprise … we'll be fine."

Taffy leaned into him in a silent gesture of encouragement.

Benny licked the frosting off his fingers and whispered in her ear, "There's enough dynamite under that pew to blow half the church into the Mahoning River. It's all good, don't worry."

That night, they lay in bed intertwined with each other. Taffy kissed Benny on the mouth and ran her fingers through his hair.

"This is going to be our last night sleeping here, right?" she asked.

"I think so. If it goes as planned, we'll have to scoot right after everything goes down."

They lay in bed, listening to the mills and the trains, the constant clanking from the huge machines, the constant whistles and horns. Neither one spoke for a few minutes.

Finally Taffy cooed, "Will you fuck me? One more time in your bed."

She kissed his neck, and they fell into bliss, one last time.

Carmine got up with the sun, kissed his wife goodbye, and left for an early-morning breakfast with the head of the steelworkers' union in Youngstown. That meeting would be done by nine, and then he was off to Our Lady of the Rosary to meet with a city councilman to discuss the upcoming county elections. From there he was off to see his mistress and spend the afternoon with her drinking wine and playing gin rummy.

After his breakfast meeting, he stopped and got a newspaper, then instructed his driver to head to the church. The car rolled up to the curb, and Carmine stepped out.

"How long you gonna be, boss?" Charlie asked.

"Not too long, Charlie. Just hang tight. Go park the car and read the paper," Carmine said, scanning the parking lot.

He walked slowly up the stairs and into the church. Nobody was in the large sanctuary but him.

He sat down in his usual pew and sighed. He gazed up at the gothic ceiling and chuckled, thinking Catholicism was a racket run by the *pezzonovante* for time immemorial. Unlike many of his fellow Italinas, he rarely went to church. He was dismayed that good families who struggled to put food on their table would, every Sunday, give what little extra money they had to the church. He shook his head wondering how many more gold chalices the church needed.

From time to time he would attend a wedding or a christening, but this was rare. It was at the last wedding he attended that the idea of using a church to conduct business first occurred to him. As usual, the clever Mancini found a use for the church and cleverly extorted it.

This would be the last time he did business in this church. Just the slightest hint of infiltration by the FBI was enough for Carmine to abandon the church. He was reasonably sure the FBI had yet to figure out his motivation for coming here, and he doubted Gallo was able to get the FBI to act before the Centofanti girl killed him. For now, he felt he was safe, but he would take no chances.

Benny and Taffy sat in her car across the street. They had parked in the lot of a set of row houses that during the day were mostly empty. The occupants all worked in the mills, and if they weren't busy making steel, they were day sleeping, resting for the night shift.

Taffy carefully parked between two other cars and blended in perfectly. In Benny's hand, he held a remote device he had constructed using the bits and pieces from an old transistor radio and what he could gather from Mancini Construction.

"When, Benny?" Taffy asked, nervously.

"Now. Whoever he's meeting isn't here yet. I guess that's good," he said.

Benny craned his neck and was able to see Carmines bodyguard, Charlie Whippo, sitting in the driver's seat of Carmine's Lincoln. He was reading the newspaper and was lost in his own world.

"You ready, baby?" Benny asked, breathing heavily.

"Uh-huh," she said, crossing her legs. She had just peed her pants but barely noticed.

Back in the sanctuary, Carmine pulled out his pocket watch and sighed. He was early, but to him that was already late. His father used to say, "Carmine, even if you on time, you already late."

He smiled thinking about his father; it was the last thought he ever had.

Benny flipped the switch, and the back of the church blew out, not a boom, but a KA-WACK. The entire back of the church launched itself across the back parking lot and down the hill. Bricks, glass, and pieces of Carmine Mancini cascaded across the parking lot in a tidal wave of destruction. Taffy screamed and covered her head as the shockwave blew out windows for two square blocks. In the blink of an eye, not only the back of the church was blown out, but all the windows and one of the front walls were destroyed, too.

It began raining chunks of wood and bricks for a square block almost immediately after the blast. A piece of stained-glass window flew almost a quarter mile and ended up skidding across Federal Street, hitting a parked car, and blowing out a tire.

Four months after the explosion, the tire shop that was two streets away needed a new tar paper roof. The first morning the crew started work, a young roofer named Jeff Biggio stopped short and looked down and blinked his eyes in disbelief. At his feet was a semirotted forearm and boney hand. On the pinky finger was a large gold ring laced with rubies. Jeff licked his lips, and using the tips of his tar-stained fingers, he carefully and repulsively pulled the ring off and put it in his shirt pocket. He then looked around quickly and called out. "Hey! Fellas! Look at this!"

After the explosion was over, and the debris was finally settling, Taffy slowly began to drive away. The witnesses that were there didn't notice the car leaving the scene. Their eyes were glued in disbelief at the carnage in front of them.

"Benny, holy shit," she said, laughing.

"Holy shit is right," he said, wide-eyed.

As the pair drove down toward the center of town, they passed a parade of police and fire vehicles.

"You're a little late, boys," Taffy chimed.

Benny chuckled, reached over, and tapped her crotch. "You had a little accident."

Taffy looked down. "Shit, I did."

They drove back to Benny's loft knowing they were relatively safe. The family would be occupied with current events, and anything dealing with Benny and Taffy would be on hold for the time being.

He pulled his car into the garage and locked it. Benny walked in first and made sure everything was OK inside; he then went down and got Taffy.

"I need to jump in the shower," she said feeling slightly embarrassed. She went to the bedroom and grabbed a change of clothes and turned on the shower. A half hour later the pair was sitting on the roof looking down at the dirty, oily city below. The wind was blowing hard, and the smell of iron ore drifted across the roof.

"What now, we just leave?" Taffy asked.

She was looking out over downtown, and slightly beyond was Our Lady of the Rosary Church, or what was left of it. There was virtually no smoke or fire. What little smoke there may have been was instantly mixed with mill smoke and carried east where it would pollute towns east of Youngstown.

"We should go. Is there anything in your apartment you want to bring with us?" he asked.

She sighed. "I have everything I need packed. Anything else I need, I can buy."

He nodded, looking out over the city with her.

"You OK?" he asked.

She dropped her chin, and the tears silently came. He lifted her chin and looked at her. "Baby, it's going to be OK, we'll be OK. Carmine is dead, baby. That means they are rudderless; we have one thing on our side right now, time. Now let's get our shit together before they do. Even with Carmine dead, it'll take Lou and Dominic about five minutes to put the pieces together and figure out it was us."

Taffy nodded, wiping away the tears. "OK, baby. I need to make a stop or two before we scoot for good. Is that OK?"

"Anything you want, Taffy, anything you want," he said, holding her face gently.

CHAPTER 44

GOODBYE, BRIER HILL

They drove in silence through the cemetery. The gray Youngstown sky was laced with bands of dark smoke from the mills. Taffy looked up into the sky and rubbed her eyes as Benny maneuvered the car into a small gravel pull off and turned the car off.

"I'll wait here, baby," Benny said, squeezing her hand.

Taffy nodded quickly, opened the door, and walked through the perfectly cut lawn to her dad, where she stood in silence for a long time.

"Pappa, I have to leave. Maybe forever," she cried.

It's OK, Taffy-girl. I understand.

"I love you, Daddy."

I love you, too. You be careful. I worry about you.

"Don't worry about me, Daddy. I have Benny, and he won't let anything bad happen to me."

OK, Taffy. You remember your daddy loves you more than anything. I see you one day, and you get to meet your mama. She loves you too.

"I probably won't be able to come see you anymore. I hope you understand."

Oh, Taffy. It's OK. I'm always with you; you know this. You can talk to me anytime. Your mama, too.

"Thank you, Daddy."

She leaned over and gently kissed the top of the headstone. "Goodbye, Daddy. Taffy-girl loves you."

Benny pulled up to a payphone, and Taffy hopped out. She quickly dialed a number she knew by heart and looked around for anything suspicious.

"Little Soda Shoppe, this is Moe," the voice answered.

"Moe, it's me. Listen carefully; go out the back door and meet me at the corner of Ada and Victoria. I'll be there in five minutes. Don't tell anyone where you're going, and make sure nobody at LaVilla sees you."

"OK. OK, Taffy, I'll be right there," she said, confused.

Five minutes later Benny and Taffy watched Moe running through the alley clad in her Soda Shoppe uniform. Taffy jumped out of the car and ran to her.

Moe fell into Taffy. "Taf, what's up? Where have you been?"

Benny watched the pair but couldn't hear what they were saying. He watched Taffy grab her by the shoulders, talking very quickly. They both were in tears. They embraced for a long minute, then Moe ran back through the alley.

Taffy jumped back into the car, crying hysterically.

"You OK, baby?" Benny asked, touching her knee.

She nodded her head quickly while looking down at her feet

and continued hysterically crying. Benny gunned the engine and pulled away with his hand on her knee.

Benny's GTO roared through downtown, over the Market Street Bridge headed south into Boardman, then farther and farther away from Youngstown. Inside the trunk were a few personal items, both their birth certificates and Social Security cards, two suitcases with clothes and toiletries, and a duffel bag full of cash. They rode in silence as the scenery went from urban, to suburban, to rural. Their minds were both close and far away as the scenery of haunted-looking farmhouses, pink flamingos, and corn silos flashed by like a strange nickelodeon. Taffy tried to take everything in that she could. She smiled looking at the cows and big green tractors in the fields. This was her third time out of Youngstown since she was thirteen, and this new technicolor world bled color and life like she had never seen.

She had on a pair of oversized white sunglasses and a Pittsburgh Pirates baseball cap, turned backward. The sky was so blue it hurt her eyes to look at it. Her long black hair swirled and danced in the wind as Benny guided the convertible down the rural roads, still heading south. She unbuckled her seat belt, took off her glasses, and slid over next to him. With her arms wrapped around his neck, she kissed his cheek.

"Baby, I love the fuck out of you, you know that, don't you? Tell me you know, Benny. Tell me," she pleaded, teary-eyed.

His grip on the wheel loosened, and he pulled the car off the road into a small dirt patch, next to an impossibly huge cornfield, and turned off the engine.

He held her face in his hands. "There ain't no going back now," he said to her.

Quickly and desperately she screamed out, "I don't wanna go back, Benny. Never, Benny … Never! Never! Never!"

They held one another in a desperate display of unity for a world that they created and ultimately destroyed. Behind them was a life that neither one was prepared to live, but both were prepared to leave. This was a chance to wash away the sins of their lives and start again. An opportunity that they would take no matter what.

She wiped her tears and blew her nose into a clean tissue. She looked down and smiled. Clean snot, watery and clear, not a trace of steel dust or dirt. She put her sunglasses back on and adjusted them. With a deep breath of finality and closure, she looked at him, "Ti amo da morire, Benito."

He smiled. "Ti amo da morire, Taffy."

The red GTO slammed out of the turn off and headed south to a brighter future—a future where a sepia world did not exist. A future where the best sound Taffy and Benny could hear was the hum of a lawnmower engine and the crash of the waves, far away from Youngstown, far away from Brier Hill.

THE END

EPILOGUE

Less than a year after the assassination of Carmine Mancini, the Sheet & Tube company laid off over five thousand steelworkers in Youngstown. Three weeks later, Republic Steel laid off forty-five hundred workers followed by US Steel that completely closed its Youngstown plant, putting more than seven thousand men out of work. Union greed, the inability to modernize the ancient plants, government regulations, and foreign steel dealt the Mahoning Valley a blow from which it would never recover. The effects of the layoffs were immediate and widespread. The local newspapers called it Black Monday, the day the city of Youngstown died.

After the shock and dismay had ended, the mass exodus of people from Youngstown began. Families moved south and west looking for work, and it seemed as if everyone had a relative somewhere that had a job waiting. The ripple effect was astonishing. The mills closed; the bars and taverns that lined Poland and Wilson Avenues quickly followed suit. The housing market plummeted while the banks struggled to sell the foreclosed homes and businesses. The city plummeted from two hundred thousand people to sixty thousand in a few short years.

With the Mancini family now rudderless, the organization crumbled under infighting and strife. Lou Santisi suffered a stroke less than a month after the death of Carmine Mancini. While sitting at his kitchen table, reading the morning newspaper and nibbling on his toast and eggs, a red film seemed to cover his vision. He collapsed on the linoleum floor in a heap. Ten days later, he died.

Dominic Capetti lacked the charisma and leadership ability to take control of the family and set affairs straight. He was able to instill fear into the soldiers but was never able to earn their respect. Dominic was an effective negotiator and strategist, but his inability to lead disqualified him from anything more than an aide to Carmine and Lou. Dominic saw the writing on the wall after his lifelong friend, Lou, died. He retired and moved from Brier Hill to the small village of Lowellville, just outside of Youngstown. Dominic died in 1988 from brain cancer.

Carmine Mancini made the critical mistake of not foreseeing the closure of the steel industry in Youngstown. Carmine, like most of the people and elected officials, assumed the good times would last and last. Carmine was not alone. Many of the institutions that did business in the city were blindsided by the events of Black Monday.

The loans and debts that were accumulated from the steelworkers, store owners, and gamblers simply dissolved. The debtors moved away, and the sportsbooks closed. With the death of Carmine Mancini, the influence of public officials disappeared almost overnight.

Benny and Taffy simply drifted away into history, along with many thousands of other residents of Youngstown. No red flags were raised when they disappeared, and as far as anyone was concerned, the young couple simply left for a brighter future, a fact that wasn't too far off from the truth.

Moe never saw or spoke to Taffy again. Two weeks after the chaos around Brier Hill began, she received paperwork from an attorney in Florida. It was signed paperwork giving Moe the Soda Shoppe and the building. She eventually sold both and moved west, settling in Phoenix where she met and married a trooper with Arizona Highway Patrol. They had three children and a wonderful life together. Moe died in 2004 from lung cancer. The small, malignant cell had become infected many years earlier from a deep breath she took in Brier Hill while playing stickball. In the last days of her life, with her family at her bedside, she asked her husband to find an old photo album in the back of the closet. With her husband's help, she slowly turned the yellowing pages until she came across a faded photograph of her and Taffy embraced in a hug; they both had huge smiles on their faces. The photo was taken on opening day of the Soda Shoppe. Moe sobbed hysterically as she held the picture close to her face. Two days later, she died. At her funeral, her husband, Doug, gently put the photograph in her casket to be buried with her.

Ralph Testa stayed in Youngstown and took a job building Chevys out at the Lordstown Chevrolet Plant, a job he found endlessly monotonous and tiresome. Sometime around 1987, a fed-up Ralph packed his belongings and headed west to California, where he hoped for more sunshine, more girls, and a better life. He landed a job with the Santa Monica street department and eventually worked his way to supervisor. No one could have imagined the life that Ralph had left behind in Brier Hill. The nice guy that ran the street department was once a lynchpin in an organized crime family a million miles away.

LaVilla Pizzeria was bought by Grace Baptist Church in 1981 and by 1987, it was abandoned, and eventually the building was condemned and set for demolition. Before the wrecking ball could level the building, a group of mischievous teens started a fire on the loading dock in the back. The fire quickly ran away with itself, and the building burned to the ground.

The Catholic diocese closed many of the churches in the city for budgetary reasons compounded by the dramatic drop in population. One of the churches that avoided the ax was Our Lady of the Rosary, which was rebuilt after the 1977 explosion and reopened in 1979, and it remains open to this day.

By 1993, Brier Hill's forty square blocks were mostly wrecked and dilapidated. By 2000, most of the neighborhood buildings had been demolished, and the city partnered with Millcreek Park to turn huge areas into green spaces. By 2020, the old Brier Hill neighborhood was just a shell of its former self. The block that Taffy and Benny grew up on was nonexistent. Every building had been razed by the city and, sadly, many of the lots had become dumping grounds for tires and garbage. The few houses that remained were tilted and looked hexed and haunted with high grass and broken windows.

On a chilly and cloudy fall afternoon in 2023, a new Cadillac SUV with Florida plates slowly drifted through the old neighborhood. The soot and smoke that once blanketed Brier Hill was long gone, along with the constant train horns and sounds of the mills. The car stopped in front of an open lot on Turin Avenue littered with tires and sporadic garbage. The grass had not been cut in a very long time, and it blew in rhythmic patterns in the fall wind. The sky was iron gray and cold as a light sleet began to fall.

A man and women stepped out of the car. The woman wore big designer sunglasses and a black retro Gatsby hat. Her white hair blew in circles around her face. The man walked in front of the car, and she quickly grabbed onto his arm.

"We did the right thing, didn't we?" she asked in a sort of pleading tone, taking off her sunglasses.

"Yeah, baby, we did," he said, almost absentmindedly.

The woman sighed and began to sniffle and cry. In the distance they could hear the wail of police sirens.

The man looked over his shoulder at the vacant lot behind him with a wisp of a smile on his face that exasperated his age lines.

He gently pulled her close, and they hugged on the dirty, cracked, and broken sidewalk—the very same sidewalk where so many years ago they had walked hand in hand. The same sidewalk where they had both played stickball and where she had held her daddy's hand.

She wiped her big blue eyes. "I still love the fuck out of you."

He smiled and said, "I still love the fuck out of you."

Made in United States
Orlando, FL
10 August 2025